Ends of th

Ian P Buckingham

GREEN CAT BOOKS

FIRST EDITION
First Published in 2020
by GREEN CAT BOOKS
19 St Christopher's Way
Pride Park
Derby
DE248JY
www.green-cat.shop

Ends of the Earth

For Mark, Jane and Tait.
Thanks to John and a special mention for Skyla, Zahra and
Loveday from beautiful Porthleven for their creative work in
naming Matisa.

CONTENTS

Introduction

This is the second book in what has become known as the changeling saga.

In the first, **Legend of the Lost**, readers were introduced to the ancient Trelgathwin line (aka the Savage family).

Following an evil curse from the maternal grandmother, who jealously disapproved of the union of her daughter with James Trelgathwin, the family were cast adrift in a black magic storm that transported them through time and shipwrecked them in two halves, wiping their memories.

The families only re-learned of each other's existence following the chance discovery of magical artefacts and powers that gradually drew them closer.

As if assembled by a magical force, they were all summoned to battle with a malign threat to nature, the worlds of the fae and the human race.

Mistakenly, they fought one another. They were saved by love.

Now, having re-connected, their enchanted journey continues.

Book 1:
Changelings Depart

Just as Henry thought he was in real trouble, mind racing for a plan, the agony suddenly eased, and the weight lifted from him.

Looking up, he could see his attacker rising into the air, as if flying. It then disappeared, end over end, into the dark landing with a loud yelp and sickening growl several feet away.

Before he finally blacked out, the last thing Henry saw was a stream of purple lights. It was like the tail of a falling star dropping spectacularly against the backdrop of a pitch-dark African night. And at its centre was the smiling face of his sister.

Farewells are so much harder when you feel like you've only just said hello. But that was just what it was like for half the family as they had to wave their other half off at the posh, Victorian station house.

The fateful battle of Berkhamsted Castle had threatened but then reunited so many members of the Savage, or ancient Trelgathwin clan. It had been traumatic. But they were slowly healing together, and they had just spent the long winter and soothing spring as one, at last.

This had been a wonderful time of fireside chats, invigorating walks with JJ, the delighted and heroic terrier, a time of holding hands and healing hugs. It was a magical period of catching up and re-learning about each other as they reconnected as a united family for the first time in too long a time.

This slice of history was like taking a large, refreshing gulp of fresh love after being lost for too long in a barren desert of selfishness and spite.

They had now finally shrugged off the malevolent dark forces. They were starting to heal together as they bathed in the warmth of each other's stories, hopes and dreams. Yes, they were all finally dreaming again and without the darkness falling upon their chests and poisoning their innocent ambitions.

But inevitably, just as they were relaxing back into each other, life had thrown them fresh challenges. Which is what life has a cruel tendency to do.

Sadly, the most sensitive felt it first.

Savannah's mystical Mer-kind light had gradually dimmed. She was living too far inland from the sea. The short days and long nights had taken their toll on her, despite how hard she tried to stay positive. Without the crisp water to refresh her changeling soul, the pollution we all accept as normal now in our inland towns clung to her. They could all tell that she really needed to return to the fresh and cleansing tang of salt air, coastal sun and sea spray. She was, of course, fond of the family home here. But it was too far from the crystal cave in Cornwall.

Their mother had also withered noticeably and more than James, their pops had feared.

Watching his wife closely, as was his way these days, he noticed how at times she was incredibly happy surrounded by the children and husband and the life and love and light she had forgotten. During these brighter periods, it was clear that she was so distracted that she genuinely appeared to be unwittingly lost in the moment, simply soaking up the affection that had been lost to her for so long.

Then at other times it was as if a great, dark, corvid crow of mobbing sorrow fell suddenly, its force suffocating the good. It didn't look like evil, more like a pandemic shroud of self-loathing, doubt and guilt conjured generations ago.

In this state it seemed that she was isolated, alienated by the shock of it all and the paradoxical way she felt. She was waging a private war with the evil influence summoning her from the shadows. This trapped her in her thoughts, making it hard for her to leave the refuge of her room without discomfort. It was as if the weight of what they had all missed when apart, pressed down heaviest on her shoulders and the sorrow was catching up with her like a mythical dream hag, a night monster extracting a sickening price.

She sighed a lot. She became paranoid and complained that their friends and family were "looking down on her" or "were suspicious". She was also becoming physically hunched or slumped. Her mousy hair had turned mostly grey, she drew a shapeless, colourless coat about her person, even in warm sunlight. She secretly clawed at herself and wielded a protective scowl to keep dangerous questions at bay.

Although the children couldn't take her troubles from her, as much as they wished they could, they went out of their way to counter the sadness that crept out from within their mother.

But her depression was often there, like the sharp talon of a sadistic raptor toying with the frightened field mice of her fleeting happier thoughts.

It frightened the family.

James privately feared that some of the poison from the tainted Firehills had attached itself to her. Worse still, he worried that perhaps her own mother's dark magic had leeched into her soul and taken up permanent residence there.

But of course, he shielded the children from those concerns.

Try as they did, with each passing day, the children found it harder and harder to cheer their mother up. But nevertheless, they put on impromptu magic shows, entertaining recitals even composing random silly songs.

The family was also visited by groups of faerie folk from Ashridge Forest and the surrounding countryside who, from time to time, brought magic and delight. This included a group of militant squirrels and glis glis now acting as the furry guardians of Berkhamsted Castle, who became very firm friends with Henry.

Sprites and talking beasts appeared with treats and tributes and proud tales of regeneration in the woods, now that the poisonous mines had been cleared.

Woodland birds, like pigeons and doves and gaily coloured pheasants sometimes landed for lengthy conversations, proud of the season's fledglings they brought to meet these now legendary names, the forest's special changeling guardians.

But while their natural and supernatural friends restored a slight sparkle to their mother's eyes, as her own children stretched their glittering wings and joined birds and bats to sample the joy of the sky, seemingly nothing anyone could do sustained her spirits for very long.

Typically, in the end, it was Nanna Jo who suggested a remedy.

"A holiday!" she cried. "That's what we need. A holiday. It will be grand," she said in her cheery way, dismissing the sceptical looks of her son.

"I'll take Savannah, Lucy and JJ with me down to Mermaid Cottage in the Leven, for a good dose of sun, sand and sea air. We can meet yer friends down there, as usual," she gestured to the younger girls. "Then, of course, we can spend time with Nelson, Ziggy and the rest of the gypsy pirate clan."

It was excited giggles and wide smiles all round at the mention of their colourful and loyal companions from Porthleven, Penzance, Kynance, Marazion, Coverack, the Lizard and Mousehole.

"Ah, the true motive. A chance to see Greybeard again, eh?" James teased, winking.

She dismissed him with a snort before finishing outlining her plan.

"THEN that frees up yer dad to take up that university lecturing trip to Africa for a few weeks with yer mum. Change of scene will do 'em both a world of good and he should get on with some work too."

She beamed as she spoke with her usual sunny disposition.

"Oh! But what about me and Holly and Henry?" piped up Alice, hands on hips, never one to stand on ceremony and always one to stand her ground.

Her fair hair was as tousled as usual, freckles prominent and her cheeks flushed. She had been playing with a brace of white weasels on the lounge rug, who paused when they sensed the change in the tone of her voice.

"Well, you shall come with us, of course," said her mother, cutting through the tension as she suddenly loomed into their large, wooden panelled living room, wrapped in that old grey woollen shawl, as if cold to the bone.

The shade seemed to follow her in this big house.

"Won't they, darling?"

She grimaced as if finding those words hard to utter, but smiled at her husband as if both seeking and affirming confirmation.

James was pretending to read in a large green armchair in the corner. Glasses perched on his nose. But he had been listening, as always. He smiled indulgently in return. He then took off his specs and replied in a balanced and considered tone, feeling all eyes on him as he spoke.

"What an excellent idea. A decent break. Some relaxing time. Then we will all be back together again in Hertfordshire ready for the harvest festival. To celebrate the full recovery of the forest."

The excitement bubbled out of the children all at once, voiced, as ever, by the raven-haired Holly.

"Can we really come with you both, Daddy? Really?" She almost launched her wings with the excitement, despite not wearing her Rubyrobe, such was her delight.

"And do I get to visit Savannah's cave with JJ, Mummy?" asked Lucy, jumping up and down with her sister, while JJ ran around and round their feet, barking with delight.

"But of course you do, darling," her mother said, a warm but ominous smile on her face, which seemed a little forced,

11

Savannah thought, her own skin beginning to tingle at the prospect of seeing the sea.

"All the dangers must have passed by now."

So, on the back of that announcement, fast forward just a few short weeks later and they found themselves gathered, with multi-coloured duffle bags, cases and ride-on Trunkies packed, saying their farewells at the train station.

Thus it was that, despite vowing never to be separated again, one half of the special changeling family came to be heading to London then west to Penzance and the wild and wonderful Cornish coast.

The other was set for Heathrow Airport and a working safari in deepest, darkest, dangerous but deliciously exciting Africa.

There was a tinge of sadness at having to say farewell again. Perhaps it was a portent of what was to come? But mostly they were all bubbling with an irrepressible sense of adventure. For they were now the Savage family, still of ancient warrior stock and they would always be together, whatever kept them apart.

So, before they knew it, once again, the air was charged with the promise of legends to be made, crackling with enchantment and singing with the possibility of the sort of unseen surprises this unique group now knew only too well.

The first thing you notice about Africa, especially when you travel from Europe, is the stark difference in the colours. It starts, as most things do, with the light, the plant life and the patterns of the land.

As Holly gazed out excitedly through her oval plane window while her siblings devoured their oddly rubbery breakfasts, she could see miles and miles of shades of brown ground beneath them.

Unlike their homeland, where so many people are packed into a relatively small, green and blue space, here she could easily imagine herds of nomadic animals wandering the vast plains they were passing over. The very thought of millions of wild things sent a thrilling tingle down her spine. And, true to character, she had been doing her research, reading up voraciously on the animals and indigenous people.

What followed when they landed was even more stimulating and surpassed all expectation. It was a whirlwind in a kaleidoscope of fabulous sights, sounds and smells as the family set foot on the continent of origins for the first time.

As they collected their bags at the exotic sounding Windhoek Airport, they were met by a man who seemed to be one giant walking smile.

Moses Matwetwe was the family's dedicated guide for the extent of their trip. And there can surely be no more enthusiastic a representative.

"Welcome to Africa and warmest greetings from the ancient peoples of Namibia, my land," he beamed proudly, simultaneously gathering bags in wing-like arms and ushering the excited family to his huge safari vehicle.

The children had eyes the size of saucers during the lengthy drive to their desert dune ranch. It was so exciting, it ached.

They were thrilled to pass small groups of colourfully dressed women selling craft wares along the side of the dusty roads. These statuesque ladies had their babies swaddled in technicoloured blankets on their backs and seemed to carry their body weight in goods balanced on their heads. Yet they all waved and cheered enthusiastically as they drove by. This was despite the fact that they threw up a thick fog of dust and stones in the car's wake, like a speedboat on dry land.

The children spotted antelope, giraffes and wild horses en route. Each was heralded by a scream of delight and frantic tapping on the car windows or a sibling's shoulders. They even spied a shining snake the breadth of the road slithering in a tree and at one point had to stop and wait for a troupe of huge, fierce-looking baboons to finish drinking from a trickling riverbed.

When they eventually managed to navigate the shallow stream in a rare valley ford, Henry shouted his excited disappointed at not seeing any crocodiles in the brackish water.

This made Moses guffaw hilariously, for Namibia is famously one of Africa's driest lands.

At various points on their trek, groups of ostriches appeared to race the car. Much to their delight they actually managed to keep pace with them for quite a long way. Their long necks were bobbing for some time before disappearing into the dusty tail of their land cruiser.

And at one stage, the girls saw what they thought was a rat run across the road before them, only for Moses to correct them with a mildly sinister smile. For it was, he explained, actually a spider the size of a man's hand and it was easily big enough to eat a small bird. A chilling thought for the faerie folk with many tiny friends.

Very few vehicles shared the rough roads with them. So, it wasn't a surprise that the few amazingly higgledy piggledy shacks and dwellings they passed seemingly made from the land itself, offered "tyre and windscreen" changing services. These were advertised on exotic signs made from shiny hub caps, stones and what appeared to be real bones. They were in the middle of the baking hot desert, after all and here resources were as precious as the people were adaptable.

It was a very long drive and despite the luxury of the air conditioning and cold drinks, Holly was the only one who managed to remain fully awake when they pulled into the entrance to Solitaire Farm, their isolated bush camp. She was delighted, but then recoiled slightly in disgust at the pool of dribble the snoring Alice had left on her shoulder.

Sunset was falling fast, yet the quality of the light here was still breathtaking. It reflected off the rust-coloured soil like an old map and filled the sky with a purply-orange hue that was both soft, threatening and embracing.

"An African hug of a horizon," Holly muttered breathlessly.

They had all woken now and yet the beauty of the sunset stunned them into ongoing silence.

Despite it seeming arid, the terrain teemed with life. They could hear some but there was so much they just couldn't yet see.

Colourful guinea fowl came out to greet them and scattered like grumpy plump aunties as the four-wheel drive truck pulled into the welcome oasis. Then, at the crest of a hill that framed the pretty camp, a majestic beast, crowned by javelin-like long, straight horns, was suddenly silhouetted against the setting sun.

"Wow. Look. An oryx, our first!" Holly cried breathlessly, shaking her siblings more awake and pointing up at the hill through the large sunroof.

"Look. Up there. You're missing it."

But when Alice and Henry rubbed their eyes and eventually focused sleepily where their sister pointed, all they could see was the shape of what looked like a man retreating from a hill in the distance. He was bearing what appeared to be two long rods, or perhaps spears.

Before the still-waking children could point out what they thought they had just witnessed, their smiling hosts, clad in khaki and deep tans, came out to meet them enthusiastically.

First, they embraced Moses in the manner only people with long and close relationships do. And then the blonde and weathered husband and wife team of Danie and Candice (Candy to her friends) Du Toit, greeted them all in turn with warmth and trays of very welcome refreshments.

Alice was especially thrilled to see that both their hosts were wearing brush/veld-coloured long shorts and safari shirts with lots of utility pockets. For khaki safari gear had been her own personal outfit of choice. She smirked at her siblings knowingly, who doubtless regretted their teasing back in England as much as they regretted their long sleeves and soon sweaty trousers.

"You don't get style like this in Primarni," she scoffed.

Having grown up, mostly isolated and home schooled, in a cabin in the woods, Alice was making up for lost time on the fashion front and took every opportunity she could to change. Every day was a dressing up day for their sprite sister, the most complex of the changeling clan.

It helped that the many pockets in her outfit also provided lots of hiding places for her very special, magical friend, her animated wand. He was purring reassuringly near her breast, or possibly snoring.

"Wonder when they last saw a dragon in Africa?" Alice thought to herself, smiling.

Their amazing safari accommodation was all they could wish for. The thatched, mud-walled rooms were a delight, the smell of the veld grass filling the cool spaces and their greedy senses. Four poster beds fringed with mosquito nets and showers open to the moon and stars made the children squeal with delight. They even managed a quick dusk swim before dinner, taking turns to pay tribute to their mermaid sister as they swam through the spotlight that exaggerated their movements.

"See…. Savannah would have been ok here," Henry joked, as he squirted a jet of water through his jagged teeth at Alice, so often his sparring partner. They splashed each other enthusiastically, droplets hissing on the stone slabs surrounding the pool that still retained some of the intense heat from the desert day.

Meanwhile, at the edge of the rippling light cast by the pool lamp, the night creatures already snuffled and sniffled away at their nocturnal morning chores, doubtless searching for their first meal of the long scavenge for survival in extreme conditions.

Dinner for the people that night was a feast of a stew cooked on a huge campfire in what the local folks amusingly called a poike. This was a bulky, potbellied cast iron pot.

At first it reminded Alice and Henry of something they had grown up with back in the forest cabin, one of a witch's essentials. So they viewed their food with trepidation, checking it for a bat wing, root or rat tooth.

Judging by the amused twinkle in their mother's eye and her first suspicious sniff as they were served delicious contents from the pot, the similarity with her cauldron had not been lost on her either. But she smiled when she spotted that her children had clocked her reaction. Then she tucked into the scrumptious meal as the night folded them all in its comforting embrace, witnessed by a million starry, starry eyes.

Their first African evening passed in enthusiastic and excited banter to the backdrop of hypnotic singing by the farm camp team. Their language was magically lyrical and their enthusiasm so catching that soon the children were all on their feet joining in what was called the long snake dance. It involved them connecting to the person in front of the line by holding their elbow and then moving to the rhythm of the clapping hands, in unison, like a human ripple.

While their collective shadow cast on the wall by the orange of the campfire was impressively serpent-like, predictably the children struggled to stay in sync, especially Henry. This was much to the amusement of their parents and their fellow guests. Werebeasts, sadly, aren't renowned for their dancing feet, not even the friendly ones.

The thrills were coming thick and fast, as no sooner had the dancing ended but, armed with torches of real fire, Moses took them on an amazing, impromptu nocturnal hiking safari.

The first discovery was that, here, in the bush, it was truly darker than the darkest part of the darkest cave in the desert at night.

There was nothing but the moon and stars to guide them and when they held their torches up to the brush and trees, sparkles from a myriad of watching eyes flashed back at them. It took what was left of their excited breath away and was all the girls could do not to spring their own wings and fly into the bushes to greet their curious hidden hosts.

At one point during their careful nocturnal hike they even saw a cheetah, in silhouette, for a few teasing seconds as it sat atop a large termite mound before slipping silently into the darkness when the group approached.

But the absolute highlight for Henry was on their way back when they stumbled across a huge rock python. It had made its wicked way, via a giant termite mound up a baobab, or upside-down tree.

"She is hunting the weaver birds," Moses explained, and just as he did the air burst into life with a mobbing crowd of angry, pecking parents.

They watched the battle for a while, secretly concerned but relieved to see them wear the predator down and send her on her way.

"They are very clever how they build a huge nest together. The entrances to their nests are very hard to access and they work together as a team, like a feathered village. In Africa, many times the animals show us that no matter how small, the little ones working together often win."

The family all smiled at this story. It was something recent tough experience had taught them only too well.

As they trekked back in single file to their rondavel and canvas accommodation in high spirits but rather weary from travel, Moses said something, in hushed tones, that made the hairs on the back of their necks stand on end.

He stood motionless, framed by the weak silvery light of the moon when he issued this whispered warning, "Tonight, before you sleep, you will notice that your beds are raised higher by a pile of bricks.

"Well here, our sangomas, our witch doctors, use powerful spells to protect our guests from the night walker. We call him the Tokoloshe. This demon comes up though the boma, sneaking from the stream."

Suddenly all three children broke rank and were gathered round Moses as they walked the last few hundred yards in slow step with their guide.

"Ticklishy?" enquired Alice, with a gently mocking giggle in her voice.

But Moses stopped and suddenly his tone changed. Now his demeanour was very much more serious.

"No, the Tokoloshe is NOT something to laugh at, children. If he bumps his head in your room, he will surely take revenge. To start, he will bite off your toes and…"

They could see the passionate light flicker in his eyes, perhaps catching an ember from the still-burning campfire, or perhaps something more?

But then a sharp voice cut through the dark, nipping him off in mid-flow.

"NOW, Moses, let's not disturb our guests with talk of such native superstitions, hey?"

They hadn't noticed her, but Candice was standing on what she called the stoep, a large veranda by the communal bar and braai or campfire area.

"But YOU know...." his voice trailed off as he saw the expression on her face change.

The camp owner smiled at their guests reassuringly after darting a conclusive look at her friend.

"Boys and girls, we raise the beds on bricks simply because it is one of many quaint traditions of the people here.

"It dates back to the times when we all camped outside, and we didn't want to be on the floor with the creepy crawlies like spiders and scorpions.

"Who would?

It's simple really."

She clearly felt the tension, which possibly hadn't been much improved by her explanation as she then laughed and added,

"Of course, nothing like that can get into your rondavel huts now, so you have nothing to fear."

Surprisingly, their host noticed a look of disappointment flash over their faces.

The boy Henry barely left a print when he walked, almost cat-like in his grace outdoors. Holly seemed to have a confident aura about her that grew as she now pulled a rather grand cloak about her shoulders. And could that have been something glowing and moving now in Alice's breast pocket?

They seemed to be an extraordinary bunch. Yet how was she to know that these changeling children were not just naïve European kids but part of a quite extra-ordinary, magical family?

And how could she know that these very special guests were to change the fortunes of her ancient native country, and the planet, forever?

After the most excellent, rejuvenating night's sleep, back in the quiet bosom of the ancient land of everyone's ancestors, they were all up with the peculiar chorus of the African dawn.

In this corner of the globe, dawn sounds very different to the crowing of the European cock, the traffic noise at rush hour, the phone alarm or the ever-present digital radio or tv.

As soon as night gives way to light here, the frogs and crickets hand over to the insects of the day. They create a clicking choir as a backdrop to the heat that swells as surely as the rolling coastal tide.

After a truly delicious breakfast of exotic fresh fruit including guava, melon, bush apricot and pawpaw to accompany their cereals, they grabbed a packed lunch and were soon back in the four-wheel drive car with the grinning Moses in the driving seat.

"Today I am taking you to a very special place," he announced in hushed tones. "It was once the sacred gathering spot of the

San people, an ancient tribe of nomads believed to be some of the first people of this earth."

"We're going to see the rock carvings, children," said their father from the front passenger seat.

He couldn't conceal his own excitement, as he would be including the relics in his lecture to the university later in the trip.

Pops had donned his khaki gear, long socks and bush hat and winked at Alice over his shoulder as he spoke.

"Ohhhh, Daaaad," was the common cry of the children, however, who, it seemed, were less enthusiastic about some old drawings than he had hoped.

All the adults laughed at this response, but not wanting to disappoint the children, James added,

"Well, I'm told there are plenty of animals on the way and some even claim that there is an elephant graveyard somewhere nearby."

That earned the sharp collective intake of breath he had hoped for.

Elouisa, however, noticed that Moses was surprisingly quiet when James said this. A bit of a surprise for one so chirpy and incandescently bubbly.

They made a quick pit stop at the evocatively named Solitaire garage. It was a splendid oasis decorated with skeletons, the rusting hulks of abandoned vintage cars and trucks, half-buried in sand. Here they stocked up with provisions, lots of drinks, car sweets and surprisingly, incredible pastries including rusks and very messy koeksisters, like long yum yums. Then they were soon back on the long and winding dirt roads.

An hour into the journey, their car approached a shape moving fleetingly ahead against the hazy horizon. As they gradually got closer, they realised it was a large and graceful antelope, or deer that was running by the side of the man-made path. It was unlike the horned monarchs they knew from home. Seemingly stronger and somehow wilder, it was clearly skittish and very fearful of this unwanted encounter. It was galloping for all it was worth and despite its grace, power and beauty was clearly distressed.

Moses slowed down until the car matched its speed so his passengers could admire it. But to the sensitive children it somehow felt wrong to add to its anxiety.

"Kudu bull," he announced with pride.

"See its beautiful markings on its flank, large ears, strong muscles and magnificent head of curling horns? It is a trophy much prized."

"Trophy? What do you mean?" snapped Holly.

"Well, hunters…."

But Moses was abruptly cut off as he began his answer by a sudden shout from behind the driver's seat.

"WATCH OUT!"

The proud and noble animal had clearly had enough of running. It suddenly veered across the road in front of them.

Moses slammed on the brakes and only just managed to halt the vehicle in time, as it skidded sideways through the sand on the road to a sharp stop.

The buck advanced slowly now, eyes fixed on them. It then took up a defiant position in front of the car.

It scanned the passengers. Then it settled eye contact on the worried face of the driver.

It began pawing the ground with its hooves. This buck clearly wasn't frightened any more. Something in its manner suggested the opposite, possibly anger, as if it recognised something disturbing about the passengers in the car. It held this pose defiantly, as if daring them to advance. As if challenging them to follow.

Then, without realising what he was doing, Henry instinctively put his own head out of the window. He sniffed the air, a light breeze coming from behind and ruffling his blonde hair.

Suddenly the attitude of the buck changed.

It flared its nostrils, flicked its large ears, snorted indomitably, violently then tossed its head back wielding those mighty twisted horns like curved sabres.

Finally, it charged the car.

Somebody screamed.

After a few long but rapid strides, the buck veered away at the last second. Then, with a mighty bound, the mighty bull scaled the fence on the far side of the dirt road in a single leap.

"I'm so sorry," a sweating Moses eventually announced to a car filled with pale-faced Europeans, who had mostly instinctively ducked down below their seats, including a rather guilty and sheepish-looking Henry.

"Is everyone ok? I have never seen a wild antelope behave in that way before. They are normally very, very shy of people."

He was relieved to see that no harm had been done and all passengers were now smiling nervously. So, after a few reassuring words and a knowing look between one young boy and his concerned mother, they were soon back on track and leaving lengthy dust clouds in their wake.

The incident ended as abruptly as it began. But all three children had started to feel a tingle in their stomachs they really hadn't thought they would feel again.

The nervous smiles exchanged between them suggested that today's innocent trip to the far side of the great dunes could prove to be a lot more significant than any of the family had first thought. And it was a sharp reminder that, with this special group of people, the promise, or threat of magical adventure was never far away.

Sossuvlei is home to the largest sand dunes in the whole world.

To the children, these huge caramel mountains of soft desert sand were as high as London's greatest sky-scraping towers. Can you imagine mountains of sand of such gigantic proportions? Like standing in London's Parliament Square, but where everything was made of earth. The dunes were simply awe-inspiring in every rusty shade of burnt orange and amber. And here they were, tiny people, blinking and gasping together at their towering magnificence.

Even before Moses could issue warnings about snakes or scorpions or the sweltering desert heat, his guests had left the car's air-conditioned comfort and were already running up the side of the dunes. They seemed oblivious to the power of the morning sun, which created a wavy heat haze everywhere they looked.

"Burrowing spiders, reptiles, lions, watch…" but he realised they were already too far and could only look pleadingly to their parents instead, while waving his arms.

They both smiled indulgently and watched with a sort of nervous pride.

As the sand was indeed scalding, the siblings were pleased to have donned their Veldskoenes, a sort of soft, suede boots that their mom had picked up at the airport shop in Johannesburg. They were perfect for moving through soft sand.

Alice had opted for a yellowy natural tan to complement her safari outfit. Her baby dragon Willowand had, of course, loved the multiple pockets which it explored with relish, eager for a shady vantage point to check out the action. Holly and Henry, on the other hand, chose purple and blue respectively, colours that jarred a bit in such a stark landscape, but which looked fabulous, all the same. The desert shoes gave them purchase on the sand because of their wide base, like camel's toes. They also kept their feet cool and protected.

When they got to the summit, breathing hard, Africa suddenly seemed to open up before them. They looked over and into a huge bubbling and dancing ocean of rusty gold and shimmering, scintillating heat as far as the eye could see. They were being rewarded for their climbing efforts by a sight that wouldn't have changed for millions of years.

Not a single man-made thing came into view, nothing artificial at all.

It was amazing to think that at one time, this had been a great river and these sands part of the dried riverbed herded into piles by the strong, dry and relentless African wind that had long usurped the water.

Here and there, dotted about the landscape were small herds of animals. Although what they found to eat, or drink here puzzled those not in the know.

Not one to miss a fresh experience of such amazement, Helygen, Alice's Willowand now sat unnoticed on her shoulder. It had taken the form of a reptile, basking in the Namibian sun, as if it had been born here.

"Look at him, "Holly laughed, pointing.

"He's turned the colour of the sand, like a funky chameleon."

"You never stop amazing me," Alice chuckled, tickling him under his chin until he puffed mini clouds of smoke from his nose, in the same way a cat purrs.

They enjoyed several minutes of awe-struck silence before the adults finally approached. This sent Helygen scuttling shyly into one of Alice's pockets as he always did when the witch or strangers approached.

Moses was a bit out of puff when he arrived at the summit. Despite breathing heavily, he still managed to point out the route the migrating animals have always taken when trekking to find water or scarce grazing.

"If you look far to the left, between what seems like those huge hills on the horizon, they were riverbanks once. Well we are heading to a valley down there. It is there where the ancient ones settled.

"It is so beautiful," exclaimed Elouisa, breathless herself now, but with amazement at what appeared to be a large flock of fuchsia-pink flamingos flying by almost at eye level, on their way to their home in the distant salt pans or shallow riverbeds. It was noticeable that she was in her element in the heat. While the others covered up, she had now loosened her blouse and removed her hat.

"Indeed, it is," her husband said, placing his arm tenderly behind the small of her back, in a soft but supportive embrace.

It always thrilled the children to see both of their parents sharing an intimate moment after the troubles they had all had to endure. Parting had been a painful sorrow for them all, but especially their parents who had to carry the burden of the re-awakening thoughts of what used to be.

Their father, who seemingly had more dark magic resistance than his children, had clearly never had his memory as badly wiped by the wicked enchanted storm that forced the family apart on that fateful night many moons past. So he had felt the loss of his children and partner most acutely as a result. Alienated from them, but still tantalisingly within reach, alive in memory and dreams. Those years had tortured his waking and sleeping hours. He was a changed man for what he had endured. But he tried hard not to let it show. He seldom looked back now, and he was always focused on the family's future.

Their mother's ongoing confusion, on the other hand, stemmed from a mixture of prolonged exposure behind the veil of the dark magic her mother had exposed her to and the unnatural, polluting force that threatened to take over their forest home. She was recovering still. But she seemed to be in constant turmoil as if the forces of light and shade ever raged within her, competing for dominance and control.

So, for their little family to have a moment of unity like this, orchestrated by such ancient wonders, was the stuff the children's dreams were made of.

While the girls were feeling the intimacy and romance of the moment, all Henry, who was an altogether more primal soul, could think about was what it would be like to morph into his were-form right here and now. There was something primitive about this place, that was taunting and teasing and enticing him to slide then run down the side of the dune and to join with the animals below.

Because his power was more bestial than that of his sisters, he was prone to fits of wild fantasy from time to time. They were all still getting used to them. Back home he had been known to go on "extended walks", especially when the moon was full and the sky clear. The muddy trousers and berry stains on his face and hands on his return were always the giveaway.

It was Moses, however, not Henry who broke the spell of the beautiful moment. He gestured toward the sun and motioned that they had better leave before they burn to a crisp.

"Man, this weather would boil the blood of a lizard."

Alice felt her pocket stir as he said that. But thankfully their guide never noticed.

So, reluctantly, the small group retraced the footprints they had made in the virgin sand on the way up and the children half ran, half surfed the huge dune, making it down in a fraction of the time.

But as they did, no-one thought to look up.

For if they did, they would have seen a large group of what appeared to be carrion vultures circling on the thermal currents up above them.

This was a signal that something had either just expired or was very near to dying.

And it appeared to be rather close to where they had left their safari van, their sanctuary.

Cornwall was twinkling, and Porthleven in particular, was alive with crackling carnival fever as the Savage family's home group arrived back at their beloved Mermaid Cottage, snuggled along the harbour wall.

Inside, as usual, everything was just as they remembered, from the blue and white striped tea services and crockery down to the multi-coloured fishing nets on painted bamboo poles waiting patiently behind the front door.

Their famous arch above the entrance, a trove of "found things", shone brightly in the late afternoon sun. And the large lump of polished ruby sea glass tried its best to make up for the Moonstone which now permanently adorned the necklace about Savannah's gracious neck.

Her complexion had transformed noticeably with every mile travelled closer to the sea and now her skin had the gentle glow of fresh Cornish clotted cream.

The day was too far gone for the girls to head to the beach for long. So they chose to run Jack out to the edge of the harbour wall, past the old clock tower, the town's famous sentinel and then to clamber out on to the rocks by the surfer's paradise area.

They grabbed a purple and a red net from their store and then headed for the door while Nanna Jo finished the unpacking. As they were about to disappear, she just had enough time to shout,

"Remember 'tis the big beach barbeque tonight so be back before dark...."

But then she smiled to herself to see them so content, especially as this was their first time back to this special place since being reunited.

The tide was out now, so the girls were able to readily clamber through the rails onto the rocks, although they were as slippery as ever.

Out beyond the break water, belly boarders were still trying to get some late life out of the sea, but it was a fairly calm and tranquil day.

Lucy had not taken the Ravenring off since it claimed her. She was twiddling it on her finger in a preoccupied way as she walked, her strawberry blonde locks falling over her eyes. Her hair had become a deeper copper since the bonding and now she too glowed with confident health.

Savannah, ever sensitive to the moods of others, her sister's especially, smiled and put an arm about Lucy's shoulders.

"OK then," she said gently.

Lucy looked up into her sister's kind face and replied.

"Really? Can we?"

"Yes, but we shall have to be quick. You heard Nanna."

But before she could finish the sentence, Lucy was already sprinting across the sand toward the secret location of Savannah's crystal cave, JJ in hot, excited pursuit, yapping his guttural glee.

It didn't take the girls long to reach the magical curtain of vegetation that marked the slender boundary between their two worlds.

That veil is much closer than most people, especially adults, realise. If only normal people still believed and knew where to look.

Upon stepping through the curtain of sea grass and back inside, the rosy glow returned to Savannah's cheeks, like a turning tide. Within seconds her clothes had fallen to the floor and she was gliding effortlessly through the azure water in her beloved cave of crystals.

Lucy, on the other hand, stood with her mouth open, hungry eyes trying hard to take it all in.

"Better to close your mouth, Sis," Savannah teased.

"Don't want to let ALL the sand flies in."

She had forgotten that only Holly had been here so far. Lucy only knew about this special place from the girls' stories and Savannah had clearly forgotten the impact of the beauty of her sanctuary. Recent events had given even her a refreshed appreciation for the serenity of this special place, but nothing could match the impact of a first encounter.

Stalagmites and stalactites sparkled like polished jewels or even light sabres, changing colour with the different waves of sunbeams that splashed on them through the fissures in the granite and serpentine walls.

Mingling with the jade that radiated from the seaweed on the walls beneath the line of the tide, the air had a distinctive green glow and the absolute freshest of scent.

"This is what underwater must look and smell like," Lucy spluttered without realising she had spoken out loud.

"Well, sort of," Savannah chuckled, tickling a friendly blenny on the snout as it popped its head out of a rock pool to see what all the fuss was about.

"Perhaps we'll be able to show you this holiday?"

Then she looked up at the far cave wall, noting the last few fingers of reflected sunlight on the back wall.

"We can't stay for long. Remember, we did promise."

As she spoke, her eyes were drawn to her sister's hand as she slowly raised it to her face. She was gazing in awe as the Ravenring was pulsing and giving off, if it were possible, a strange dark forcefield of inky light.

"Lucy, your hand."

"I know," her sister replied.

"It's the ring. Something is wrong."

Both girls now stared aghast, as the magical relic that had adopted Lucy of its own accord, now morphed into life.

The raven stretched its wings, jade eyes burning bright. Then what followed, she could only describe as the sensation of becoming a puppet, a marionette, as someone or something raised her arm for her. It was her ring taking control. Next, she was inadvertently pointing behind where her sister swam.

The map wall containing the Legend of the Lost, Savannah's famous magical painting of their family's saga, was now shrouded completely in a dark cloud.

Slowly, the mist dissolved into a sequence of pictures, a sort of storyboard, with their painted avatars coming to life on the cave wall like an animated film or cartoon.

First, figures that were clearly their father and mother appeared to be in a state of distress standing near a pile of huge grey boulders.

Meanwhile, images of their sisters fought and wrestled with what looked like a crowd of angry, dark shapes that appeared to be carrying away the hog-tied body of their brother, Henry. They were heading through a forest of dead trees toward a smoking mountain or volcano in the distance.

But when they looked back, they could now see that the boulders had trunks, and large ears and were in fact, elephants. What they thought was a pile of bones next to them turned out to be what those elephants were quite clearly missing. It was a pile of their abandoned tusks.

Then out of nowhere, a large golden bird flew into the picture, circled a few times and then turned and headed straight at them. As it grew and grew, they could see that it had a grotesquely painted, human appearance, a look of fury on its face until, at the point where it would have reached them had it been real, it suddenly burst into a rainbow of falling stars.

The black smoke then wisped and curled like a nest of angry, savage serpents. It was bubbling, if smoke can be said to.

When the chaotic swirls started to take shape again, the next scene depicted the sea and Savannah's domain.

A family pod of orcas, killer whales, the largest relatives of dolphins on the planet, was clearly hunting a school of fish. Silvery scales were glinting as they were panicked by the vast dorsal fin of the dominant bull and cow and their pack.

But just as the orcas closed in on their prey, the scene shifted again, the black smokescreen descended. And when the next frame took shape, it was a shocking sight.

All the orcas appeared to have beached themselves, stranded on what looked like a dried-up seabed shore. About ten of the family members were lying in amongst rocks, shells and the carcasses of other sea creatures, a feast for the hungry gulls.

On a hill, overlooking the scene of desolation was a crooked figure in a black hooded cloak, a wizened old woman in what looked like a wooden cage and a younger man who, to their horror, had fire pits for eyes. Above him, a black bird raised its beak, opened it and swallowed the bodies whole.

Then the black curtain quivered, formed itself into a large raven -coloured mass for a few heartbeats before it dropped and disappeared as fast as it came.

Holly was typically the first to react to the scene and take the initiative. After first making sure she was out of Moses, the guide's eyeline, she dipped beneath a dune and summoned her cloak. She did this with a concentrated thought, as she had now learned to do.

She had lain her Rubyrobe loosely on top of her expedition rucksack. It wriggled free and in no time at all landed snuggly about her shoulders, like a second skin. After another quick glance about her, she eagerly pressed the ornate golden clasp. She was greeted by the familiar tingling rush of her transformation, like being pulled backward through a rainbow and was soon flying up to where the huge birds were circling.

This fae changeling had never had the pleasure of meeting vultures before. In fact she wasn't sure whether any fae existed in Africa at all.

These were fine specimens of the carrion bird species.

But they sensed an easy meal.

"What are you circling above our car for?" asked Holly, luminous wings glistening, as if it was the most natural thing in the world to talk to a mob of dangerous scavengers with an array of incredibly powerful talons and beaks. She had reduced down to her faerie size, but her voice and other attributes retained the full range of her human form.

"Your car, insect?" coughed the bald leader incredulously in a husky, threat-ladened squawk of a voice, as he cruised lazily on the thermals on long, languid wings.

"What need would one like you have for a man-horse?"

"It's a filthy changeling. fae!" shouted a marabou stork who had just joined the winged gang, his distinctive, massive, bald red head and white legs making him stand out from the other scavengers.

"Catch it! You vultures were too busy drooling over the nearlydinner to see it changing down there where the other snacks are."

"Nearlydinner?" repeated Holly, in a sufficiently puzzled tone, to earn hoots of mockery in bursts of fetid breath she could even smell this far in the air. She sensed she was too fast for them but felt uneasy nevertheless.

"Yes," croaked the stork, clearly amused and a bit irritated as they started another circuit.

"Haven't you seen poor old Dinganwe? That massive grey cluster of tough t-bone steaks?

"He's on his last legs down there and he needs to get a hurry up and die. Some folks is hungry and we'ze mouths ta feed at home."

Holly stopped circling the thermals with the carrion crew then dropped a good forty or fifty feet.

There, by the side of the smaller dune to the side of their safari truck, she could indeed just about make out a shape, largely obscured by the dune's shade.

To the backing of the derision of the chorus of vultures, she sped over to the stationary shape and as she got closer, she was amazed to have missed it.

Elephants may be Africa's largest land mammal, but they are surprisingly good at not being seen, when they don't want to be. A useful trait that many potential prey beasts share.

Ask anyone who has been on a viewing safari and they will tell you how frustrating it can be at times as, with their stone and dust-colour, like the air itself, elephants sometimes disappear into the surroundings. This is especially true if they have caked themselves in mud.

Well this large fellow, and fellow his massive frame, huge ears and large tusks signified he was, happened to be doing a pretty good job of blending in.

Yet the vultures weren't easily fooled.

Holly flew down and alighted on a branch of one of the rare, hardy trees to survive in this arid zone.

The elephant looked up at her with very small but very sad, milky eyes. It wasn't angry at all, but rather seemed resigned to its fate.

Then she saw it, the nasty looking wound on his huge shoulder.

He had been shot.

"Oh you poor, poor thing," she said in a soothing purr of a tone. "Whoever did this to you?"

At first the great beast said nothing. But then he gave a huge sigh, exhaled through his trunk and said slowly in a deep, sad, sonorous voice,

"The poachers did this. The filthy tsotsi attacked my family. The others got away, I think. But I have come here to look for the elephant's graveyard. I have come here to answer the final call."

Holly couldn't believe she had heard anything quite so tragic in all her young days. And given recent events in her family's history, that was saying something.

The elephant went on to tell her that his name was Dinganwe and that he was resting in the last of the shade before continuing on his great trek, his ultimate path.

Holly had now changed her position and after asking permission, was seated on one of his long tusks. This way they could speak more easily without causing him more discomfort having to raise his head.

She felt the shiver of tension rise as he sensed the proximity of the others in her party before even her fairy senses had time to tingle.

"Don't worry, my friend," she whispered soothingly. "We're all here to help where we can."

When her siblings ran over, naturally Alice was amazed and a little frightened to see an African elephant so close up. As for Henry, well, he was in awe so kept his distance in case he was giving off any…predator wolfie scents or vibes.

In no time at all, her parents had sprung into practical action, as they do, and accompanied a completely flabbergasted Moses to the car. He was finding it hard to string together a sentence.

"But an elephant…a bull…by the tree…squash us all…we must…..the children…why don't we run?"

James just smiled and reassured him. He decided to distract him by keeping him busy. Soon they were reluctantly unpacking the iron poike pot they had brought along for the bush camp dinner later.

Meanwhile, his wife scoured the area for the local herbs and minerals she would need to supplement her own supply. She kept this in her now famous Everbag, a constant source of amusement for the children as her strange draw-string purse, while only small, seemed to have endless room inside.

Soon, while Holly (back in human form), Lucy and Henry kept their new, special friend company, administering some well-directed scratches on thick hide, Elouisa lit a fire and had an interesting smelling brew on a rolling boil in the metal poike cauldron.

Moses was now reluctantly preoccupied with setting up camp and he and James undertook the task of erecting the two great canvas structures with the cooking area in the centre. He was still casting nervous, furtive glances backward, however.

As it happened, they were in an incredibly distinctive lunar landscape of a spot. Like nowhere else on earth.

There were perfect circles dotted everywhere in the dirt here, a regular pattern as if painted by aliens. Moses had said that the local people called the area the Leopard's Land, and the marks the "spoor" or "footprints of the wind".

"There can be few parts of the world left where a person can literally place their foot in the fair assumption that nobody else had ever placed their foot there before", thought Holly, as she watched several small herds of antelope wander past through the heat haze, serenely oblivious to their presence.

"This place is truly, truly amazing."

Even the blood-sucking carrion birds gave up the ghost eventually and retired to roost on a dead tree. So the omens were looking good when Elouisa, after muttering a chant under her breath, finally skimmed the scum off the boiling potion and filled a bowl with the steaming, noxious liquid.

She then mixed this with the soil taken from one of the perfect sand circles, chanted another incantation and then smiled to signal that it was ready.

Moses, taking a brief break from camp-making, watched what he now decided was a powerful white witch, with a mixture of fear and respect sketched on his face.

But Henry was keeping a wary eye on him. He had grown up with this sort of magic and he knew how unsettling it was and how normal people often distrusted Wiccan-kind.

He noted that Moses had now taken out what appeared to be his phone and looked like he was secretly filming. So, he wandered over to the guide, as noiselessly as were-kind are blessed to be when the will takes them.

"Whoooa!" exclaimed Moses, when he eventually noticed Henry, so suddenly but stealthily, so close and now watching him.

"Does my mother interest you?" Henry enquired in a breathy tone, teeth glinting ever so slightly as he smiled, a gesture intended to calm him, but which served only to unnerve the worried man further.

"Well.......it is not every day that one gets to see...."

His sentence trailed off as if he couldn't think what to say for the best.

"Hm!" said Henry, pausing for effect, then nodding at the phone.

"So probably best we keep this to ourselves, no? Not sure it will be good for business otherwise."

"No. I mean, yes! You are right, of course. Um...shall I make tea, Mister Henry?"

The were-boy nodded and smiled that smile again and their guide set to work, nervously rustling packets and clanking cups.

Meanwhile Elouisa, with the help of her daughters, had formed the unctuous medicine into a paste and they were tenderly covering the elephant's wound, cleaning it out as they did.

Holly and Alice morphed into their faerie forms to get to the tricky bits. This didn't seem to surprise the mighty Dinganwe at all. He even kneeled in response to their gentle requests and seemed to giggle with great snorts of trunk air, if elephants do giggle, when they got behind his ear.

Before long, as dusk approached, their charge gave a massive bellowing sigh and seemed to settle into what, for elephants, passes as deep sleep. He simply locked his leg joints and ....dozed off.

"That will be the goodness in the potion working," smiled their mother.

"Used to have the same effect on you two. Although I have had to change the recipe a bit for the weed-like plants they have here.

"Of course, he's also a bit bigger than you two."

She laughed as she said this, recalling some special times back in the Ashridge woods, raising the children, before the great remembering.

Their mother's joke set all three of the changeling children into fits of laughter.

But as they fell about, this happened.

Night had fallen suddenly, as it does in Africa, like a dark wave crashing on rocks.

Lit only by the glow of the flickering fire, nobody had noticed that they had attracted attention.

Lurking just beyond the lick of the glow from the flames, a dozen pairs of eyes had encircled them.

The pack of hyenas had been drawn by the scent of blood and decay as the family cleaned their new friend's bullet wounds.

Henry was the first to detect the change in the air. So he quickly, but firmly, ushered the girls towards the protection of the fire.

His father noticed his son's actions and motioned to Moses with two fingers to look to the dark.

He did so just in time as, somehow, as if coordinated by a silent command, half a dozen sets of teeth attached to slavering and snickering jaws hungrily, if nervously, inched forward.

James quickly pulled two flaming branches from their fire and armed himself and Moses. They formed a triangle around the girls with Elouisa taking the third point, her own branch-like wand drawn, its tip glowing ominously.

Henry, however, was a step ahead. Realising that they were being lured into a distracting trap, he ducked between the adults and sprinted back towards the elephant, ignoring the panicked cries of his parents.

He could hear, behind him, his family giving a good account of themselves as he ran. From the bursts and flashes of light he suspected that Alice's Willowand was at work with its pure, Pagan Wiccan magic. He knew she would be flanked by the protection provided by their elder sister Holly and their mother, each bringing their own distinctive fae powers. But, despite the pyrotechnics, he couldn't afford to stop to look.

He was changing into were-form as he ran. He arrived just in time as the rest of the hyena gang were almost upon the drugged elephant, their main target, as it slept.

Without any attempt at subtlety, Henry smashed crudely into the gang like a ferocious bowling ball of fur, sinew and bone.

Two monsters were knocked into the dark, yelping like scalded pups. Another two, seeing the fate of their mates, turned tail and ran, for although hyenas have the strongest jaws in Africa, capable of crushing the toughest of bone, they are crafty and cowardly and put self-preservation first.

One, however, much larger than the rest stood its ground. Here was a beast who had the marks to prove that he had faced down lions in his time.

The shape of his jaw gave him the appearance of the smiling Joker from Batman or a malevolent clown, Henry thought. He especially didn't like the look of the huge scar that ran the length of his face, right across one eye.

"Vell, wot haf we here?" he snarled, in a tremulous voice both deep and high-pitched, with a sort of laugh at the end.

"Sum sort of a doggiewoggie maybe?"

He dribbled and spat as he spoke, anticipating a meal with his fight.

"But I theenk I vill jus call you our DinnerDog."

He was taller at the shoulder than in the hind haunches and very muscular in build.

Like all hyenas, he had the look of a distorted, pumped up, dirty bear, not unlike the mutant animals in his mother's former forest army.

"Why don't you come and find....?"

Henry didn't get to finish the sentence as, faster than expected, his opponent gambolled across the few feet separating them, and with a snickering scream, seized him by his shoulder. He would have taken him by the throat had Henry's were-reflexes not saved him.

The two fell into an apparent death roll, with Henry howling in pain, while clawing at the hyena's jaws with his free arm and claws and sinking his own fangs into the scruff of its mangy neck.

But its hide was tougher than expected and it tasted absolutely rancid, greasy and putrid.

Just as Henry thought he was in real trouble, mind racing for a plan, the agony suddenly eased, and the weight lifted from him.

Looking up, he could see his attacker rising into the air, as if flying. It then disappeared, end over end, into the dark landing with a loud yelp and sickening growl several feet away.

Before he finally blacked out, the last thing Henry saw was a stream of purple lights. It was like the tail of a falling star

dropping spectacularly against the backdrop of a pitch-dark
African night. And at its centre was the smiling face of his sister.

Savannah was so shocked by the revelations of the Ravenring on the walls of her crystal cave, that it moved her to tears.

She only hoped that the sight of the stranded dolphins, whales and elephants was a warning of action they needed to take and not a premonition of what was definitely to come.

Judging by her pale face and open-mouthed expression, Lucy was very shocked by what they had just seen.

The darklings had retreated back into the ring and it no longer glowed with power. It was so annoying that they now had been alerted to a problem, an unnatural, natural disaster. But for now, it was a puzzle, without an answer and many missing pieces.

Savannah glided splashlessly across the magical pool to join her sister and their terrier, who was tilting his head in confusion at what had just happened.

The first words from Lucy's mouth were a surprise.

"Mousehole," she said inexplicably.

"We have to go to the village of Mousehole. That's where all of this started. It has been in my dreams. It has to hold some clues about what this means. There has to be an answer for us somewhere there."

Savannah thought for a moment, then she nodded her head in agreement.

"There does seem to be a real connection between the Ravenring and dark magick which does worry me a bit," said Savannah.

"But we know the source of that dark power, where this all started, and the time may well have come, to look into what became of Grandma after she caused the great storm."

"Hm! Nothing personal, but I just wish we had the others with us though, don't you?"

After leaving the cave together they were soon back at Mermaid Cottage, and after a brief chat with Nanna Jo, they arranged, in the morning, to catch the local bus to the impossibly picturesque Cornish fishing village of Mousehole.

Rarely has a place been so evocatively but accurately named, as the quaint little hamlet tucked cosily away on the coast.

The harbour curls a protective arm around the small fishing fleet, ushering visitors gently down to the ancient inns and cafés that line the catch landing areas.

After talking with various local folk at the barbeque the night before, Nanna Jo had arranged for them to meet a very special person down by the older dock.

Old Brinn Trelowarren had lived in Mousehole for his entire 90 years. He was one of the few natural speakers of the ancient Cornish language and Madame Rebecca, their friend and leader of the pirate clan, had recommended they start their search after consulting him.

Nanna Jo was excited by meeting up with her soulmate again and as they turned the corner, Madame Rebecca's unmistakable figure cut a rainbow dash as she held court outside of the Ship Inn, regaling a small crowd with tall tales.

As they arrived, her face lit up and soon the air was alive with purple scarves, waving arms, exotic perfumes and high spirits.

"Brinny, my 'andsome, meet our very own…" she almost used their Cornish name but had a change of mind mid-sentence, "….Savages. Yes! Meet part of the Savage clan."

It seemed Old Brinn was not the chirpiest of souls at the best of times and was even quieter at the worst.

But his face lit up, she noticed, when he clapped eyes on the children and especially when his gaze fell on Lucy's ring. In fact, he couldn't take his eyes off it, it seemed.

Sensing the girl's slight discomfort, made worse by JJ's low, grumbling growl, Nanna Jo stepped forward and held out her hand.

"Very pleased to meet you," she beamed in her usual generous way.

"We've heard so much about you. They say you may even be more famous than the 'ansom Mousehole Cat."

Surprisingly, he didn't take Nanna Jo's hand.

Instead, he rose unsteadily to his feet, muttering, "That is just a silly, silly story. Childish nonsense."

He then made his excuses and, still chuntering to himself, hobbled off, a lot faster than anyone expected for a man of his years and his reportedly friendly disposition.

"Well, oy never," said Madame Rebecca, clearly so very embarrassed, her cheeks glowed redder than ever.

"He 'ad been so chatty before and seemed genuinely pleased to be meeting you."

Looking at each other, puzzled, Madame Rebecca came to the rescue with a characteristically wacky plan.

"Nothin' for it then. We needz a long natter over some plates a stargazey pie n chips washed down with sweet, sweet zyder. Come givz me an 'and."

And with that she put an arm around the youngest and they disappeared inside the inn to place their exotic lunch order of the local speciality.

Lucy, not surprisingly, didn't look too delighted by the prospect of fish heads in pastry.

Who would?

Henry's pride was hurt much more than his shoulder, but Elouisa insisted on treating him with the same potion anyway.

"Ugh, it really smells," he growled, as she packed the wound, anxious to avoid infection.

"Not as much as you do," his mother teased.

"That hyena must have been rolling in something dead. Luckily not my favourite son."

Amazingly, their new elephant friend hadn't so much as heard the attacking hyena gang. Drugged by the potion, he was still snoring obliviously.

"Darling, hyena's mouths are filled with all sorts of bacteria and parasites. They don't brush or floss, you know. We can't be too careful. Don't want you catching something and changing into one of those twisted beasts from the Firehills, now do we?" she joked.

As she tenderly treated her son's wounds, she could feel their guide's eyes on her again.

Moses was clearly finding it hard to come to terms with what had just happened. The very special nature of his customers on this safari were well and truly out of the bag now, especially as one had transformed into a wolf, not to mention the fact that Holly had just mercilessly dispatched the lead hyena while in her fae warrior form.

James was soon engrossed in a deep conversation with the local man, and the two retreated into the tent for a lengthier explanatory chat, away from the spooky distractions of shadows cast by the flickering flames.

Holly and Alice looked at each other, shrugged knowingly and smiled.

By the time the two men returned from the tent Moses was grinning his toothy grin again, albeit a tad tentatively.

He made no further reference to the mystical recent occurrences but focused instead on preparing the tastiest barbecue, or "braaivleis" as he called it, (rolling his "r"s) that any of them had ever had.

While the family tucked into the chops, spicy sausage, or wors and the fluffy pap n sous, (a sort of deliciously maize-centred meal that you dipped into a tomato stew), they all joked about "sleeping like an elephant" that night.

But before the children eventually wound their weary way to their cosy camp beds, their mother took a bucket of glowing embers from the fire and placed a small pile at each corner of the camp's perimeter.

She swayed in a gentle dance and sang a song some recognised as an ancient lullaby as she did this, until the glowing embers formed a diamond of happy, flickering white light. It was this that protected them until the desert dawn roused them reassuringly several hours later.

By the time they had warmed up their coffee, hot chocolate and buttered the brioche rolls for breakfast, dripping with juicy peach jam, the adults had broken camp and readied the van.

Dinganwe had seemingly woken in the night. He had wandered off a little way to find something to eat.

But he was now waiting patiently and gesturing with his trunk for the family to follow.

So, led by this brave elephant prince, the unique band of enchanted travellers resumed their trek to the most sacred of the esteemed ancient African places.

Keeping the highest dune to their right, providing some shade from the sun, he directed them at a decent pace for a good twenty miles before he took his first pause.

"The potion has clearly worked wonders," Pops observed, admiringly.

"Your alchemy skills have always been powerful. But that time in the woods must have really helped you hone your special gift. There is always a positive in even the darkest of days, even though I sometimes had to look very hard for it." He smiled at his wife as he said this.

But he received no response.

She seemed distracted by something.

The children had got out of the car and were keeping their elephant friend company as he took a drink from a hidden reservoir between a group of large rocks.

"Have you noticed the way Moses now looks at me?" she asked James.

"Well, he's had a lot to get used to. Let's face it. We are either going to have to find a way to bring him into our fellowship properly or…."

"One of us will have to erase his memory at some point, "his wife replied. "Like my mother did to us?"

"Well……let's deal with that when we're forced to make that unsavoury choice, eh?"

As he said that, they both noticed the children getting a little more animated than they had been. They were pointing back in the direction they had just driven.

A large cloud of dust indicated that a vehicle, maybe several vehicles, clearly driving in their tracks, were heading their way.

"That's either very unlucky or coincidental given we're in the middle of nowhere. Or…"

"They are following us," shouted their guide, inadvertently finishing James's question for him.

"Don't be silly. They're probably just tourists on safari, not unlike us and…."

"You do not understand," exclaimed Moses, gesturing for the children to return quickly.

"Very few people know this route. It goes nowhere that tourists know. It is a secret, sacred to the elephants and only a handful of humans. This is not a casual or accidental drive."

"Well, if not, then who are they?"

Elouisa opted for the more direct approach.

But she wasn't prepared for the look on Moses' face when he said, in a hushed tone, given the children were now at the door.

"They are poachers, Mrs Savage. They are likely the same butchers who attacked the elephant. And they are here to kill him, take his tusks and to steal the legendary ivory waiting in the graveyard of his ancestors.

"The tusks of elephants are worth more to these monsters than gold. They will have guns. And they will shoot anything that comes between them and their prey, including us. Even the enchanted ones feel bullets, no?"

Mousehole was buzzing with holidaymakers and passionate people selling their seaside wares and artisan goods.

It was festival season and Pirate and Mermaid week in this part of Cornwall. So nobody really paid much attention to a small group of pirates, an undercover mermaid and a white witch wandering along the sea front.

Why should they?

For half the children heading for the beach were clad in far more outrageous attire, one even carrying a giant inflatable unicorn, much coveted by Lucy.

"There are sea unicorns, you know?" whispered Savannah to her sister, as they munched on their surprisingly tasty fish pie and chips on the bench outside the inn.

"Oooh, really?" Lucy replied.

"Yes, when people sometimes talk of seeing white horses riding the waves, especially during a summer storm, that's normally a small herd, or perhaps two playing together, especially if the sun shines from behind them."

"It would be lovely to meet some one day," she said, impatiently. "But right now, we need to get to the bottom of the Ravenring's vision. Know any friendly dolphins we can have a quiet word with?"

"But of course," smiled her flaxen-haired sibling, as if it was the most ordinary request in the world.

"I had hoped, however, that our new "friend" may have been able to shed some light on the great storm of poisons. But doesn't seem he was too keen to talk about it, does it?"

Nanna Jo caught the tail end of their chat and replied.

"Me 'n' Rebecca have got a plan. We're going to leave you kids to have an explore of Mouzll.

"Meanwhile we're going to buy Old Brinn a few treats like rum fudge 'n' stuff, and then go visit him at home, up there on the hill. We'll see if he might open up a bit more when there's bribes and a bit less of a ...crowd."

"Oh, really?" said Alice, sounding a little more excited at the prospect of them being entrusted to be on their own for a while than she had intended.

"You three stay out of the wrong sort of trouble, if you can. Have a play in the water. I'm sure not even the hunky lifeguards can match Savannah in that department, so you're in safe hands. Then we'll meet you down by the ice cream seller in two hours from now for a treat for ourselves, before we catch the bus."

With that, the two larger-than-life ladies bustled off up the street, arms as animated as skirts, while the sisters and excited terrier headed down toward the harbour wall, from where they could survey the water within the slightly sheltered bay.

Savannah, in particular, the older of the sisters, was clearly affected by the memory of this stretch of sea. For it was here, who knows how long ago, their family had been abandoned on the family boat by the villagers, angered by the terrible tyranny of their hated grandmother.

Scattered by that savage magical storm, Savannah had suffered a unique fate. She may have been the oldest, but she had been left very much on her own for a very long time, and although it was well hidden beneath her gentle demeanour, Savannah was clearly still carrying the emotional scars.

Lucy had clambered atop the harbour wall and was scanning the horizon, looking for a splash or some other tell-tale sign of dolphin life.

The only vaguely watery sound she did hear, however, came from behind her. And when she turned around to find the source, her sister had gone, leaving JJ looking puzzled, staring at a widening ripple in the calm sea

The lead battered Datsun flat-back truck, or bakkie, was crammed up front with fully loaded bad guys.

The driver was a particularly nasty looking character, with a top lip cleft, courtesy of the last thrust of the horn of an animal he had trapped. He also sported a cloudy white eye from a similar incident. This made him instantly recognisable and terrifying.

He donned what looked like an ancient tennis or squash shirt, but it had long changed from white to a manky nicotine colour of yellow. He also wore a necklace of crocodile and hippo teeth that caught the sun as they bounced as he drove.

His own teeth were filed to a point at the front, giving him a reptilian aspect, especially when he moistened his lips with his tongue. Which he did a lot.

His companions were similarly obnoxious, spiteful and cruel looking. They were all renegades from a war in East Africa, who had migrated south to live off the illegal animal poaching trade.

As their hideous convoy made relentless progress through the parched earth in pursuit of their escaped quarry, they were in brutally high spirits. Thinking they were the hunters and the object ahead their frightened prey, the malevolent band of mobsters clearly had no idea what special brand of trouble lay in store for them, waiting to turn the tables.

How could they?

First, they were suddenly plagued by swarms of biting flies that appeared from nowhere. The minibeasts initially arrived as an annoying dozen or so, climbing into their ears, getting up their noses and then their mouths, carrying whatever nasty they had just been feasting upon on their filthy feet.

Soon, however, the fierce few swelled to such a persistent plague that they started to obscure the inside of the windshield.

The filthy, battered bakkies didn't have any working windows so the bandits had to improvise, blocking the gaps using t-shirts and anything at hand. Those on the back, however, were forced to swathe their heads in rags to keep the filthy swarm of flies at bay.

Then the biting bugs arrived, and these horseflies were blood drinkers. The poachers were terrified that they may include tsetse fly that carry a deadly sleeping sickness, so they stopped the car in a panic to light a fire using the spare petrol cans.

Such was their fear of the flying menace, they virtually climbed into the flames, desperately hoping that the smoke would deter the insects.

All of this, of course, was being taken in by two pairs of shining magical eyes, a safe distance from the action.

It was some time before the poachers could return to the cars, cursing and wiping dead flies from everywhere as they clambered back on board. They argued for a while, but then, egged on by the white-eyed one with the scars, they set off once more in the last known direction of the great beast, their quarry.

Upon reaching the dunes where the family had previously camped, the driver noticed that his battered vehicle had started to pull to the left as he drove. Then suddenly the bonnet dipped and before they could think, the people on the back were being catapulted through the air, arms and legs flailing wildly like one great octopus in a hurricane.

The bandit in the passenger seat, a wild woman with a cruel laugh had just been shouting, "Faster! Make it go faster, we're losing them."

She was not wearing a seatbelt, of course, and was knocked out by the force of the impact of the car's sudden and dramatic stop.

To cap it all, as the stunned driver looked on in amazement, both front wheels, glowing a sort of green colour, rolled free and headed off into the sand in front of them. It was as if they had a mind of their own.

It was almost dusk by the time they caught the wheels and sorted out this latest catastrophe. It was incredibly difficult to dig the car out of the soft sand and then re-attach the rolling parts. They were also terrified that the bugs would re-appear or that the bewitched tyres would come to life again.

So, by the time they had repaired their vehicles well enough to proceed, the elephant and its spoor had long gone.

The men were excellent trackers, skilled at tracing animal footprints or spoor in the sand. But try as they might, they couldn't find anything for several hundred metres. All they found were some very odd marks, as if left by a broom. But it could have been no ordinary broom, as there were no marks left by the feet of any person wielding it.

It was as if the desert itself had been swept clean of tracks by someone, on what appeared to be a flying branch or branches. Someone who moved through the air.

Soon, the poachers started arguing amongst themselves again. They were scared and frustrated and desperate, a dangerous combination.

Some of them were clearly starting to fear that perhaps the stories about the mutu or powerful magic in the elephant graveyard may now be true. Others talked of devils and witches and even the Tokoloshe.

But when two of them drew knives and confronted each other, their scar-faced leader fired his rifle in the air and screamed in a shrill, cracked voice,

"Silence fools and cowards. We have elephant tusks to gather. There is but one place it can be. It is time to be rich. We go. We go on and we go now, and we do not stop until we have its head!"

Book 2:

Beware the Tokoloshe

As she drew closer to the vehicle and the promise of some shelter, to her horror, another snickering animal appeared and cut off her escape route. She was now exhausted, and she was surrounded.

When her assailants slavered and growled, she hissed and spat back at them like a feral cat, hurling curses and incantations.

She countered every lunge they made with a hand gesture of her own that blocked a snout or shut their fetid mouths with small bursts of magic energy.

But as fast as she did this, the next attack came. Then the next. Then the next. Until inevitably she felt her knees start to buckle.

Dinganwe loved listening to the stories of the children, as they described how they had sabotaged the poachers' car.

Even Henry, who was suspicious of magic, had to laugh at the way their mother had summoned the swarm of flies from a million desert oysters (dung piles, to you or me), although he could see that Moses was now becoming increasingly edgy and uncomfortable.

Their guide had, in fact, taken to making an odd gesture with his hands whenever Elouisa's back was turned. It was as if he was flicking something from his fingers or dispelling a foul smell.

"Those poachers will not give up, you know. They are tsotsi. Very bad people," he muttered to James, when out of earshot of the children.

"Well, we cannot let them reach where we are going," said James through clenched teeth, finding it hard to disguise his hatred of people like that.

"We need to keep close guard tonight, just in case, although they have no hope of tracking us in the dark."

He could tell that something still troubled their African friend but decided not to press him right now. It wasn't as if they had much choice but to use their changeling powers and gifts to survive this challenge. Unless, of course, he chose to join the poachers. But James knew people and he believed that Moses was to be trusted.

That night, the joviality around the campfire was not what it had been the night before. The battle and nervous tension had taken its toll. Although to have a wild elephant share the heat of their fire was a special type of distraction.

Mother's magic lotion had clearly worked wonders as Dinganwe's wound was no longer weeping and was healing fast. It didn't even look as though they were going to have to stitch it with the cord James had prepared, such was the was the constitution of these mighty wild animals.

While they ate another delicious bush feast, Henry mentioned that he was sensing movement and could detect flickering light the far side of the dunes. A quick scouting trip in were-form, at double pace, to the top of the highest point, confirmed that, incredibly, the poachers were still blundering on.

Given they had travelled in more or less a straight line since their last camp, it seemed that more by luck than judgement, the villains were still heading the right way.

He looked round. It struck him that it was also possible that in this desolate place, they may have seen the light from their fire dancing on the horizon.

So, to slow their pursuer's once again, Pops joined Henry with another skirmisher's plan to daze and confuse.

The boys said brief farewells and then set off together. Once they had wandered out of sight of camp, James dropped his tall walking staff to the sand. Then, placing both feet on the staff he held his hands, palms flat either side of him, and spoke the same sentence several times under his breath until the sand started to vibrate. The force of this then propelled the warlock's staff forward.

"He's snowboarding on sand," Henry laughed, tossing his blonde head back in delight.

"Come on, Henry," his dad called.

"Let's have some fun with these filth."

In lycan form, Henry easily kept pace with his father and his flying staff that he now rode with surprising ease. He was enjoying the chance to really stretch all of his legs. It also made him realise how much he had missed out not seeing his dad for so long. They were both usually so quiet and unassuming, but these were some impressive ancient skills on display.

"It's wonderful to see you running free like this, son. You must tell me more about what it feels like when you change, some day. Your great uncle was were-kind. I still remember his stories of the were-age when things were different between animals and humans. But he was taken from us too soon."

As he spoke, he forgot, however, that a drawback of were-form is that the changeling loses the ability to speak human. So he simply smiled as his panting companion gave him a sideways glance and raised what passed for a wolfie eyebrow.

They covered quite a distance, but before long the duo were positioned on a hill just above the slow-moving, battered poacher's vans.

Henry slumped onto all fours, a more comfortable position when stationary. Then he tilted his head from side to side, in canine fashion, much as you will see your own furry friends do. He was listening for instructions or gathering clues about their pursuer's intentions. They, however, were entirely oblivious to the fact that they, the hunters, would soon become the prey. Once again.

The leader of the rabble of poachers was in the passenger seat now. He had the letters PH on his back, some sort of logo that made him easier to spot in the poor light. He was half in and half hanging out of the door, scanning the ground with spotlights powered by the car.

There had been no wind to blow away the brush marks made by the girls removing their tracks and the poachers were now cunningly following this faintest of signs instead.

While Henry watched, James raised his staff and, once again, called upon the elemental spirits for help.

This time the mage summoned a sandstorm.

The bandits felt it before they saw it, gathering on the dunes. Its pulsating power swelled rapidly. Then, suddenly, breaking like the sea, it lashed the poachers with wave after wave of sand until, choking, they ground to a halt once more.

Sand clogged everything and forced the rear riders to hunker beneath sheets of plastic to get out of the cruel, abrasive winds. It also removed every sign of their tracks, submerged their wheels and created a series of fresh mini dunes that would completely confuse them by the time they attempted to return to tracking in the morning.

As James focused on orchestrating the forces of nature, Henry's attention was drawn to something odd which slipped from the car.

It happened so fast that most would have missed it, especially during the storm. But his heightened senses were ever alert.

He shook his head in disbelief but could have sworn he saw what looked like some sort of thick, white grub, or worm, a large white tube of a thing with what appeared to be legs and arms.

If you've ever seen maggots wriggling, it was like a dog-size version of one of them.

It had just burrowed into the ground beneath the car and had had now begun to tunnel straight for them.

L ucy, back in Cornwall, began to panic a little before remembering that her sister's home of choice was the sea. So when Savannah bobbed up a few hundred yards away and waved with a huge smile on her face, she couldn't help but feel relieved.

As her smile spread, a long silver missile flew through the air above her, barrel rolled with the sun glinting like diamonds on its belly and then splashed back down.

"I see she's found the dolphins," she shouted to Jack, who was now barking excitedly and pawing at the stone harbour wall.

To tell the truth, Lucy was more than a little jealous of Savannah right now. She would love to be swimming with such a wonderful creature and listening to the tales she doubtless had to tell.

But just as she said that, as if it heard her thoughts (which, of course, it did), the dolphin raced towards her and to her complete surprise deliberately "beached" itself on the cobbles near to where she was sitting. It had what she could only describe as a beaming smile on its shiny face and Lucy couldn't help but cradle its beak and get drawn into the dark pools of the dolphin's eyes.

"I am Serena," she said, speaking direct to Lucy's inner ear.

"Swim with me."

And with that, Lucy scooped JJ under her arm, dropped into the water without a second thought for her beach dress and sandals and, holding Serena's dorsal fin was soon speeding through the sea to where her sister waited, giggling with glee.

As they arrived, another two dolphins joined them, announcing their arrival with an acrobatic display of synchronised leaping skills.

Jack had wriggled free and was now doggy paddling in joyful circles. He was ably assisted by nudges and nuzzles from their new friends, who were clearly very amused by his valiant efforts to paddle ever-faster in pursuit. If he could have matched their athleticism, there's no doubt he would have.

"Is he a dog fish?" her dolphin friend laughed.

"Please meet my brother and sister, Robby and Grace. They are twins, but you can tell them apart...."

"Yes, yes, by my fish belly," chuckled Robby, in their fascinating language of clicks, squeaks, gurgles and loud exhalations of air.

"He's shy too....not," said his sister, ducking her twin as she landed.

"I take it you're here about the ruptions?"

Savannah was now mirroring the movement of the mini pod, an unspoken language that dolphins use to signal belonging.

Soon Lucy found herself doing the same, moving her body to the rhythm of their aquatic companions. She was surrounded by a slight glow as the Ravenring worked its magic, helping her adapt to the water, stay calm, and float without really getting wet.

"Well, we were here to find out whether you knew about anything amiss in the underwater world, so in a manner of speaking, yes," she said.

Lucy and Savannah then went on to relay the story of the Ravenring revelations back in the crystal cave.

For the first time that day, all three of the dolphins were still, heads bobbing with the gentle undulation of the water, but listening intently. And as she talked, they were delighted to be joined by the furry face of a juvenile grey seal.

"Sorry for buttin' in, but your conversation carried on a wave and I thought I better join you. I'm Miwky. Not a very original name, I know, but that's what the folks at the rescue centre called me on account of..."

"Your milky-white pup fur," said Lucy, probably a little too excitedly.

"Yes...Anyway, as I was sayin', I've seen the ruptions too. Nasty business. Seen a conger eel born with two heads by the outlet an' folks is sayin' it's sendin' some good sea creatures crazy...."

"That's really helpful, Miwky," replied Savannah, noticing the naughty sniggers of the cheeky twins.

"Sounds like there's something awry with the lava bubbling from the Firehills."

"Maybe worse than that," muttered the seal, most insistently. "Some sea folks is sayin' some leg folk are doin' it deliberate like......no offence meant to...." he nodded in Lucy's direction at this point.

"Leg folk az bin kind to me, like the ones at the Seal Sanctuary when my mammy got lost. But some......"

"Yes, some can be very bad, with their nets and their rubbish and their...."

"OK! That's enough now, Robby. We have guests and let's not stereotype everyone the same way for the sake of a few."

Their new aquatic friends treated them all to a last show of athleticism as they chased each other under, over and between their bobbing bodies, Savannah using this as an opportunity to flush some cobwebs from her own fins by competing with them, gleefully.

Lucy noticed that her sister was almost as fast as the dolphins, and just as graceful as the seal.

When they finally got bored with chasing each other, Lucy and Jack hitched a ride to the end of the sea wall.

They were still hidden from prying eyes and that was just as well, as folk would have been aghast to see a terrier riding a seal, nibbling on its neck while a mermaid teased two dolphins as if it was the most natural thing in the world to do.

When the fizzing trio arrived at the Cornish ice cream shop, already tasting for chunky monkey, strawberry shortcake or hoke pokey delights, they were surprised that the ladies weren't waiting as planned.

They assumed they had been detained by a particular lush cream tea or just sidelined by gossip. So the girls waited for half an hour, soaking up the harbour sights to the sound of gulls, before finally pooling their money and buying their cones.

Summer warmed their backs soothingly as they deftly worked their way through their creamy treats, while Jack snoozed on the warm pavement beneath their wooden bench, using nature's dryer.

After scattering the soggy remnants of their cones to the delight of the birds and crustaceans, the girls turned to each other with worried looks on their faces. Then they decided to re-trace their steps back to the pub where they had enjoyed lunch.

Upon arrival, they were disappointed to learn from the barmaid who was cleaning the outside tables, that nobody had seen the ladies since their last visit. However, very helpfully, she was able to give them the address of the house they had set off to visit. Oddly, however, she was most insistent that the girls should not go there alone.

"He's a queer one, that old fella," she whispered.
"Alright with the local adults n' fisherfolk but never a good word to say, 'bout Blowins, Emmits and Grockles, especially the kids."

The girls were now caught on the horns of a dilemma. But reckoning that there was only one route Nanna and Madame R could take back to the harbour, what harm could come from just popping up the hill and looking?

So, despite the reservations and warning of the barmaid, they set off at a skip up the hill.

The address they had been given was for the last house on the street. But having walked past several very pretty fisherman's cottages, they couldn't find number 13 Chestnut End on first pass and they soon found themselves facing an overgrown wood.

Re-tracing their steps, they stood with number 11 to their right and a huge hawthorn hedge. Taking a closer look, Lucy found a tired-looking green wooden gate to the side of the hedge and eventually made out the number 1 and an indentation where the 3 once was. It had clearly fallen off.

"Well," said Savannah nervously, a lump rising in her throat and flutter alighting in her stomach, "this seems to be the place. Thirteen is the fairy number, so we should be alright, shouldn't we?"

"I guess there's no point us standing here gawping," said Lucy. "We had better knock."

So, Lucy, bold as ever, rapped on the door three times. Then she tried again, harder this time.

But there was nothing at all.

Even the birds had now stopped singing, they noticed.

"Oh," said Lucy, reaching down to the base of the hedge, where JJ was snuffling at something. She then pulled out a long, translucent piece of purple material. She held it to her nose to confirm that it was, unmistakably, one of Madam Rebecca's scarves.

As they looked at each other, wide-eyed, Savannah suddenly had the creeping feeling that someone or something was watching them.

Her gaze was gradually drawn to the slight gap between the impenetrable hedge and the wooden gate.

There, behind the dirty net curtains at one of the top bedrooms, she could see what looked like two red, glowing lights. Her heart started racing as the orbs moved slowly to the left. Then she realised that they appeared to be, yes, a set of eyes of some description.

And those eyes had clearly spotted them.

Henry was still puzzling over the strange, maggot-like creature he had seen tunnel under the van, when they got back to their camp.

They were glad to see that Moses, true to his word, was keeping watch while the others slept. But it was clear that he was incredibly jittery, judging by the way he jumped when they walked into view on the perimeter of the firelight.

"Eeesh!" he yelled. "You gave me a very big fright."

James placed a reassuring hand on their guide's shoulder and quietly announced that they had probably seen the last of the poachers, at least for some time.

As a mark of confidence, he suggested that they all retire to their tents for some sleep and was amused to see that Moses didn't need to be asked twice. He soon clambered up the back of the four-wheel drive to his specialist tent pitched on a platform on its roof.

It took James a while to nod off, although it pleased him to see Henry pass out the second his head hit his camping pillow. Clearly the long run had done his son some good.

Lying on his back, it was a joy to look through the canvas and plastic ceiling window at the crystal-clear African sky at night, where myriad stars twinkled.

Amazingly, even in the desert in the dead of night, he was not the only one awake, far from it, as crickets lovingly serenaded one another and from something, somewhere, a jackal called its cubs back to the den.

James was just visualising the scene when sleep finally overtook him and he joined the chorus of heavy breathing and gentle snores.

What James had no way of realising was that the dog, or father jackal he just heard was signalling danger to his own family. For he had been out on the hunt and while stalking a dassie den, had spotted something very strange burrowing nearby, creating a trail of disturbed earth like a sprinting mole. But this was much stronger and faster than any mole he was used to.

He had silently tracked the creature for a few hundred yards. But judging by the speed it moved, he decided it must be very strong. So he chose not to investigate whether it could be food.

So, when he heard the dassie family squeaking in panic as it ploughed through their burrow, he abandoned the hunt. Instead, he set off for home and sent the warning to his family to move to higher, stonier ground.

Moses was the first to stir, as dawn broke, and he was keen to crack on with breakfast-making to ensure an early start.

From his vantage point on top of the vehicle, as he was putting on his boots he noticed that the camp perimeter seemed oddly pronounced. Yes, a strange ridge encircled what was presumably the fire's range.

He jumped down and walked over to explore in closer detail and a few minutes later was urgently rousing James as quietly as he could.

Henry's beast-sense was alerted by their guide's arrival and as he and James left the tent, Henry unzipped himself from his sleeping bag, ignored the chill of the morning air and followed.

James and Moses were on their knees examining what seemed to be strange markings, suggesting some sort of tunnelling around the camp.

But what puzzled Henry was that, as the men spoke and scratched at their heads, on top of a collection of stones marking a rare well and water source in this parched place, stood the ugliest, pig-like creature imaginable. It was scratching its hairy backside enthusiastically, at first, but when it realised that Henry could see it though the other two seemingly couldn't, it made a rude gesture with two fingers and tongue. Then, at the blink of an eye, it disappeared into the earth.

"Tokoloshe, I am telling you, Mr James, it is the Tokoloshe."

"Now come on, Moses. Here? In the middle of one of the most arid places in the country? Why would it be here?"

"They go where the badness is. They are attracted to negative feelings and evil thoughts. It must have come with tha poachers,"

Moses declared, waving his arms in an animated way that showed just how disturbed he was.

"So why not come into the camp? And, from what I understand, they have to be near water, don't they?"

Moses took James by the hand and led him over to the pile of stones.

"There. Water is there," he said, pointing to the well that James would not have seen the previous day, given his adventure with Henry.

" Oh!!" said James, peering into the dark water source, slightly nervously. "But this doesn't explain why it didn't enter the camp."

"I can answer that," said Henry, whom they hadn't noticed to that point.

"He is scared of the fire, isn't he?" he directed this question to Moses, but James answered.

"He? How do you know….?"

This time Moses replied.

"Because HE has seen him, haven't you, Mr Henry? He is the only one who can. You have seen him because of your power that comes in the night. You have seen him because he can be seen by dog-kind."

It was James' turn to become animated now, as the shock of the news of the Tokoloshe was only slightly less of a shock than the news that Moses knew more about the changelings than James had accounted for.

"Yes. I have seen him," Henry replied, only a little offended at being referred to as a dog. "And he has returned to his well now."

"But he will be back, Master Henry. He will be back."

"Listen," said James, "we will just pack up and put some miles between that goblin, his well and ourselves."

"That will not be enough, Mister James, and Henry knows."

James looked from Moses to his son with a puzzled look on his face.

"I think he is probably right, Father. He seems to be focused on staying in touch with us and I'm not sure why."

"Ah, it is because we have something that he wants, that he has been waiting for, for a very long time.

"I am the son of a sangoma; a healer, a holy man. I know these bad creatures. He has been waiting for us, waiting to increase his power. He has been longing to serve."

"I don't understand," said James, frowning.

Moses paused, measuring his next words, which he knew would cause a shock.

"He will not let us go now because he has found his mistress."

James frowned, clearly puzzled and troubled.

"He wants his witch to accept him as her slave, her minion, her familiar."

Moses' voice rose just above a panicked whisper.

"That demon, he now wants her, there. Your wife. The monster wants THEIR mother."

B reaking camp that morning happened at break-neck speed, although no-one was surprised, given the looming threat of the presence of the poachers.

Dinganwe the elephant had already set off again and made good progress by the time they caught up with him. He was clearly moving a lot easier now and was racing the sun.

Better still, despite several winged scouting missions by the fae sisters, they reported no sign of their filthy pursuers.

At moments like these, Henry lamented being earthbound and and wished he could fly as well to check for himself. He had been strangely distracted during this leg of their journey as if sensing that malevolence was back in the air, a scent last detected back in Ashridge Forest.

The terrain about them had changed quite dramatically today. Soft sand gradually took shape and eventually started to appear as sandstone hills and mountains. More and larger circles, like meteor strike points littered the landscape and the change in habitat brought a whole new rich rainbow range of wonderful animals.

Beautiful birds flew by revealing flashes of greens, yellows and electric blues. Herds of monochrome zebra gathered and clustered with families of stoic wildebeest. Despite the arid conditions, they clearly found enough to graze here as they were dotted about the plain as far as the eye could see. And the scene was punctuated by bright yellow flowers, like vibrant African buttercups.

Oxpeckers busied themselves amongst the throng. They were attentive valets at a four-legged court, plucking ticks and parasites, while here and there, groups of juvenile ostriches bobbed about comically; animated feather dusters hoovering the air of flying minibeasts and bugs.

"What an amazing spot!" exclaimed Alice, ever the keen nature lover of the group.

"We've only seen this on television before," said Holly, just as breathless at the sight of the wildest of wild animals in a truly wild and wonderful place.

Despite the strange spectacle of a bull elephant leading an odd convoy, the herds of incredible creatures barely registered their presence. Yet Henry could tell from the flicking ears of the zebra and the excited chatter and bobbing beaks of the birds that this whole crowd was ever alert to the merest hint of danger.

As they proceeded at a steady but relentless elephant pace through the dry canyon between the hills, Henry suddenly caught a glimpse of an oddly familiar feline shape on a branch on one of the trees on high.

Excitedly, he alerted the adults who signalled for Moses to stop the car and reach for the binoculars.

Pointing the glasses to where Henry gestured, he soon confirmed the presence of a watching leopard, a snoozing sentinel in the shade.

"We are very, very lucky to see such a majestic beast," he said excitedly, handing the glasses to the girls. "They are nocturnal animals, that only really come down at night when they are hungry."

While they paused to drink in the sumptuous sights, Dinganwe
had pressed on with his trek. He was clearly on a mission and these marvels, so exciting to the children, were really just his everyday world.

Although he had spoken with the family about the need to reach the sacred grounds, he had not yet shared the extent of the troubles playing on his mind. For he was carrying a heavy weight of fears. The cruel people who had assaulted him were just the start of a time of turmoil, of great trouble. That was a pressing, persistent burden.

They did not have so far to travel now. Matisa the guardian was not there just by good fortune. The leopard was the first of a host of loyal friends of the elephants who watched and guarded this ancient way.

Soon the family were spotting baboons scanning their every move and other monkeys and rodents popped into and out of sight, as if they were playing games with the travellers.

While the children believed they had caught the leopard off guard, even while he slumbered in the sun, he was in touch with the other creatures watching. Messages had already been relayed, ripples of notices and signals had been sent. For the secret of their ancient and sacred domain has been carefully guarded since the start of time and it had to be preserved at all costs.

Then, while he thought those thoughts, the great bull elephant raised his trunk in the evening air that hung heavy in the valley.

What followed was a thunderous trumpet call to herald their arrival. Its power was such that it sent the very stones to trembling.

As the children gawped in awe, all that the ever-cautious James could think about was the risk the bull elephant's call posed to the safety of them all at the hands of those listening with motives more malign.

He understood how necessary rituals like this one were. But he really, really hoped that what he could see over the far horizon was a rare raincloud and not a cloud of dust thrown up by a malevolent alien presence on rubber tyres.

Outside the creepy cottage in Mousehole, the sisters froze with fear at first. They were frightened by the sinister figure who had now vanished like a wraith from the window.

But they were mostly terrified about the uncertain fate of the lovely ladies they had come here to find.

Although it was the middle of the day and they were in a public, if quiet and suddenly deserted place, Lucy felt herself rubbing her ring finger until the raven tightened slightly.

Almost instantly, a small, grey mouse appeared from the base of the hedge, its very pink nose twitching.

"May I be of assistance, mistress of the ring?" he enquired, in a tiny voice only she could hear well. The little, polite rodent was casting nervous glances in the direction of the terrier, for terriers are notorious ratters and mousers.

Not wishing to condescend, but in an effort to be polite, Lucy knelt on one knee to bring her face closer to their new friend. Savannah, who could see what was happening at her feet, remained upright and vigilant to cover for her sister, hold Jack at bay and to reluctantly keep an eye on the increasingly sinister house.

She could hear the conversation, but she couldn't quite make out what they were saying.

After a couple of minutes, the mouse disappeared back into the greenery.

"Well, that was useful," whispered Alice.

"Our furry friend says he actually lives in the field but at times his family have ventured into the house, in the winter, when things become desperate. He was harvesting sunflower seeds in the garden when the ladies turned up earlier. Saw them go in. But hasn't seen them come out."

Savannah looked worried now.

"He has seen both an old man and an old woman living here, apparently. But he has never seen them both in the house together, which is an odd thing to say."

Lucy rose back to her feet as she finished the report of her conversation.

"He also said that it is very dark and dank, and the house seems unloved inside. The rodents don't like to go inside there because there are what he called "hunters" lurking that caught his cousin. Also, he said that there is a room in the basement that no one can get into, not even a shrew."

Savannah was thinking while Lucy spoke. She was the eldest and that came with responsibility, especially with no adults around. How she wished they were next to the sea, as she could then commune with some of her watery kind. But eventually she found her voice after weighing up their options.

97

"Well, as I see it, we can either turn around and go and wait. We can walk up to the main front door and knock loudly or…."

"We can sneak around the back via the field using the route my friend spoke about, and enter through the broken kitchen door."

None of the options exactly filled the girls with glee, especially given, up on the hill, they were too far from water to call on much help from the Moonstone's power.

But at least the sun and proximity to another familial magic item was fuelling the potency of the Ravenring. Both sisters could feel the reassuring buzz of the white magic flow between the special artefacts in their care and it felt a bit like, well, a reassuring pat on the back.

Without another word passing between them, both pushed on the large wooden gate as one. They were not thieves sneaking about in the night. They meant no ill and had done no harm and, true to the way of their family, they chose the open, direct path of honesty over sneaking round the back like cowards.

But they didn't feel especially brave as they passed though the gap in the hedge together. As they slowly stalked the crazy paved path to the rickety door with the brass knocker of a Cornish goblin's head, both sisters could feel a large lump rise in their throat, their hearts racing and the hairs rising on the back of their necks.

The small porch over the front door was virtually coloured soot-like by cobwebs. It had clearly not seen a brush or duster for a very long time.

Various gnarled creepers snaked up the columns on each side with trunks as thick as a baby's arm, their roots buckling and bulging the brickwork by the border where thorny rosebushes ran wild.

In the eaves of the awning, what appeared to be a bat roosted undisturbed in the gloom, it's droppings having stained the wall and floor, giving off an unexpectedly pungent whiff.

The windows, portals into the soul of the house and the lens to the outside world, were murky and unloved. But oddly, that knocker shone bright. It was as if grime dare not settle there. And it had the sort of face that followed the visitors as they approached.

"I don't want to touch it," said Lucy, looking to her elder sister.

"Neither do I," she gulped, "but it is just a knocker."

She reached out a tentative hand, shaking.

Then, predictably, it screamed.

"INTRUDERS! INTRUDERS!"

The piskie's face instantly came alive, with a nasty, mocking grin as it shouted the alarm, freezing the girls in their tracks.

JJ immediately started running in circles, barking uncontrollably.

Now their worst fears were confirmed.

First, they heard a fast, leathery shuffling from inside. Then before they could think to run, the door burst open with a mighty whoosh.

Suddenly, before them stood a dark, crooked, dusty, dead-smelling figure. And he had cruel anger written all over his cracked, pale and blinking face.

Dinganwe's trumpeted call alerted all the sentries to their imminent arrival. Although advance word from the leopard sentinel, Matisa, was already spreading fast.

So, by the time they took the off-path route between the upside-down baobab trees, and then through the overgrown tunnel at the base of one of the canyon walls, they emerged into the bright daylight again to a waiting guard of honour.

Everywhere they looked, to the left, right, high and low, glorious members of the animal kingdom greeted the leader of the elephants and his human guardian entourage.

All manner of cats, large and small, wild dogs, fowl, antelope, reptiles, rodents, jackals, apes and even insects ushered them into the natural amphitheatre.

You would expect a hubbub of noise, given such a gathering. But the reverence the sacred place demands meant the travellers progressed in virtual silence, compelled by the unexpected scintilla of a waterfall at the far end of the hidden oasis.

Looking up in awe, Holly nudged her sister and pointed out the arch they were heading toward, leading to what looked like some form of natural oval coliseum. As they approached, she could see that the arch was made from massive ivory tusks that must have belonged to gigantic mammoths, thought to be the ancestors of Dinganwe's tribe.

"Wow!" said Alice. "Imagine the size of head you would need to support teeth like that."

"And imagine the amount of food they would eat. No wonder there's nothing left here but the desert?"

Moses laughed and wanted to explain that had nothing to do with the animals, but before he could speak, they entered the archway of bones and he too was hushed by the atmosphere.

Dinganwe maintained a steady, reverential pace and was now walking toward what looked like a large, grey boulder. But their newly trained eyes suggested this shape was something far more precious.

When he reached the elephant, which was crouching low to drink weakly from the stream, he felt forward with his trunk and they embraced like the very old and very precious friends they were.

Moses had stopped the car instinctively, out of respect, and had paused in the shade of one of the hills near a pile of scattered soapstone boulders and rocks.

The group got out of the vehicle in silence and were clearly incredibly excited and awed by what they were witnessing.

"It's like being in a giant version of St Mary's," whispered Holly to her father, referring to the Norman church where she had been christened, the place where the grave of Peter the Wild Boy famously lay.

James smiled, however he was more than a little distracted. His own attention had been immediately drawn to an area of flat, tan-coloured rock and he couldn't believe his eyes. For there, on virtually every surface, were the unmistakable depictions of what must have been the first people and the animals that were so important to their lives. The walls everywhere here were covered in crude but surprisingly sophisticated drawings, paintings and etchings that must be thousands, if not millions, of years old. He was completely dumbstruck by the sight.

"Look!" Holly said excitedly, drawn by her father's sudden attentiveness, "is that a group of giraffes?"

"Yes," James replied, his voice trembling, betraying his excitement at sharing this moment with his daughter, the life-defining moment people first clap eyes on communication created by the ancestors of mankind centuries before.

"And over here," he pointed out, "you can see where someone has made an imprint of their hand, by spitting what they used as paint through their fingers. Like the first sprayer."

"Just as you taught us to do with paper, feathers, poster paints and straws from our craft box?"

He smiled at the comparison, realising that not that much had changed despite all the modern comforts they had.

Alice had now joined them and was laughing.

"They look like the sort of stick people that Henry draws. Funny little faces and spears like arrows."

This made her brother chuckle as she was right, of course.

"But imagine," their father announced in a hushed voice, "the people who drew these amazing scenes, like the group of women gathering fruits from bushes, had to make their own materials. They used pigment from roots and berries or different types of mud, and even ground up insect's shells or carapaces and stones. Colours like blue and red had to be discovered by crushing very specific stones or roots and mixing them with sap and saliva."

"Amazing," whispered Holly, in awe now as she stared at a scene that revealed more the more you looked at it. It reminded her, in a strange way, of the scene on the wall of her sister Savannah's mermaid crystal cave, conveying the Legend of the Lost.

"They have even captured the moon and the stars, by sticking small semi-precious stones to the sky with some sort of gum," James pointed out. "And over here, if you look, are a whole group of animals or guinea fowl made from thumb prints."

Typically, Henry's attention was drawn to the darker places, this time to the back of the sheltered area to what appeared to be a cave. So, while his family gasped and gushed, he made his way to a sandy space, his nose twitching an alert.

"What's this?" he grunted, pointing to several piles of white sticks near the back of the cave, his voice amplified by the stone walls.

The small group wandered over, slowly. But before James could answer a voice came from the back of the group.

"Those are bones. Skeletons of the people who once lived here." And while this news froze the group to the spot, Elouisa, their mother, who made the announcement stepped forward, her own eyes glinting slightly.

Clearly this latest, somewhat grislier discovery peaked her darker interest much more than the dusty caveman art.

Out beyond the break water, on the far side of Mousehole harbour, something was steadily bubbling up from beneath the seabed.

A large gang of cautious Cornish crabs had gathered together at a gap in the rocks, on a shelf sticking out from the stone ledge jutting out from a natural reef.

Given crustaceans are not averse to munching on each other, a gathering of such size meant one of two things. They had either come together to find a mate, or there was some sort of sudden and abundant food supply in the vicinity to distract from cannibalism.

The familial dolphin podlet had been playing a game of catch and throw with a plastic buoy discarded from a boat, when they first noticed the gathering.

Being naturally curious creatures, Serena left her twin siblings at their game and decided to investigate.

Rather than disturb the crabs, who can be terribly moody and more than a little nippy when surprised, she took the long route through the sea grass and kelp forest.

When she reached the end, she did her best to remain as still as possible while spying on the army of busy shellfish.

It soon became clear that they were not here for love after all, but rather gluttony, her first guess. But what she wasn't expecting was the horrific sight of the bitterly contorted bodies of small fish or fry that littered the seabed in their thousands. They lay close to where a constant stream of ugly coloured bubbles streamed from dozens of vents in the sand and the rocks.

"Poison," Serena thought. "They are being poisoned by steam from the Firehills mountains venting into the sea.

Just as this thought flashed through her mind, the dolphin noticed that some of the crabs had a strange hue. It was almost as if they were glowing. And not just glowing. By the look of those at the centre of the scrum for food, some appeared to be growing. Several were twice the size she had ever seen in this species. Their claws, especially, were now massive. And judging by the way they were quarrelling with their neighbours, despite the abundance of food, they seemed a lot more aggressive too.

U p at the surface, at the end of the long lane, two sisters came face to face with their own dark problem.

The sinister figure with blood red eyes staring at them from the open cottage door.

Instinctively, Lucy squeezed the Ravenring, and could feel surge of power from her sister's necklace as the magical streams entwined. But just as her thoughts turned to summoning the support of the dark power, he spoke.

"Oh no you don't, young lady," and with a wave of both palms in a figure of eight movement, the creepers at the doorway suddenly threw down tendrils like octopus arms. In a flash, the gnarly vines had entangled both girls.

Jack, however, was far too nimble and darted in and out of the tendrils evasively.

The surprise of the assault broke Lucy's concentration and her Ravenring spell.

"Let us GO!" she demanded, her face scarlet with rage, struggling to break free from the thick branches of honeysuckle and wisteria that were holding them fast, much more assuredly than any rope.

Lucy was now yowling and wriggling like a wild cat caught in a thicket.

"Most certainly not. At least not until I know I can properly trust the pair of you," the sinister old man said, in a cracked, husky voice.

"And you, little monster, please be silent."

With a wave of his hand, JJ stopped and sat down obediently. He submitted with barely a whimper, something nobody had ever managed to get him to do.

"What have you done with our nan?" spat Lucy, not one to be intimidated or bossed about easily, as her sisters knew well. She was also very angry at someone else controlling her dog.

"We know they came here and.....well, as soon as we get free of these....you're going to be sorry..."

As their eyes adjusted to the gloom, it became clear who their captor was. The old man was still wearing the stripy old fisherman's shirt they had seen him in earlier, but he looked so much older now.

"And those eyes." Savannah thought. "What is with those demonic eyes?" They were the sort she had only ever seen on poor drowned sailors.

He paused and turned his back on the struggling girls, then stooped to scoop up a ragged old ginger tomcat that looked about two hundred years old and was peering unperturbed from the gloom.

"Well, Skibbers. What shall we do with these nosey little twichers, eh?"

The cat meowed, as if laughing at his master's joke. But this turned to a growl as the familiar shape of an aged lady bustled through the door.

"Nanna Jo!" Lucy cried.

"Watch out for that…."

She didn't get to finish the sentence though as the plants suddenly dumped both girls unceremoniously on their bottoms on the grass.

"Now, Brinn, what kind of a Druid do you call yourself, not bein' able to drive a simple set of shrubs properly?" joked NJ, as she made her way over to the girls and helped them both up, clucking and dusting grass from their seats.

"We are SO sorry," she bustled and fussed like a mother hen. "We got to talkin' and just completely lost track of the time."

She was ushering them into the house as she spoke, an arm round both sets of reluctant shoulders.

Inside, somewhat belying what the timid mouse had said, it was surprisingly homely and cosy looking and there was a distinct smell of fresh ginger and cinnamon in the air.

"Becca's made a proper batch of gingerbread cookies. See Brinny loves 'em. We've been drinkin' tea, eating treats and catching up and….."

As they reached the kitchen, also surprisingly well appointed if a little, basic, they saw Madame Rebecca at work at the great iron range, a huge smile appearing on her face as the girls walked in.

"So, YOU found US?" she cried. "And you found my scarf. Proper job," she announced, clearly delighted. It was sticking out of the sleeve of Savannah's pretty blue blouse.

"Thank you, thank you," she cried, smothering Savannah in cloying perfumed kisses.

Their host was now busily emptying cat biscuits into a bowl as if nothing had happened. He then added half a pouch of powder to the food.

"There you go, old fella. Arrowroot, tortoise dust and lark tongue compound. That should get you through another day. Wish I could say the same for me."

He wagged a warning finger at JJ, who was edging closer to the cat and the food. This stopped him in his tracks.

The old man then emptied the rest of the contents onto his own tongue and pulled a brain-freeze lemon face, as Alice called it. He then sat down in a rocking chair, and without further ado shut his eyes.

He was snoring in seconds.

"Oh, don't be so morose, old friend," teased NJ.

"You've lived for a couple of centuries already, I'm pretty sure you'll make it to your next pie 'n' pint."

At this, he smiled and opened his eyes again. The red had all gone now, they sparkled a deep brown, almost black and his complexion had even acquired a slight blush. He looked a decade younger.

The sisters must have worn flabbergasted expressions at the events of the last few minutes, as NJ looked up at them and said,

"Girls, can you please close your cave holes? The spiders are apt to weave webs in 'em otherwise."

Elouisa's eyes sparkled as she crouched over the bones in the cave, greedily.

The dry skeletons were clearly a family group, judging by their size, their positioning and the aura they exuded.

But most importantly, she was very acutely aware of their powerful magical properties.

"These bones are thousands of years old," she whispered, largely to herself, but overheard by the children.

"Incredible. So...potent. If they were included in a potion of....."

She was about to reach out to take a knuckle but suddenly became conscious of James and their guide, watching. So she withdrew her probing hand, tentatively. Then she seemed to shake her head as she raised herself back to her full height.

"Of course, we must respect this special place," she muttered, clearly embarrassed by her actions.

"Indeed," said James, looking round at the gathered throng, as much to break the spell of awkwardness as anything else.

Henry, meanwhile, completely undetected, had been making his way further down the cave and was now examining a very odd drawing. Upon closer scrutiny, he was struck by how much the piggy or even goblin-like features resembled something they had encountered just the day before.

"Aiyeee!" exclaimed Moses, who now followed the young boy

"It is he. It is the Tokoloshe. These people, they knew tha demon."

Judging by the fact that the figure in the painting had what appeared to be several arrows protruding from it, they not only "knew" the so-called demon, but they clearly had some issues with it too.

"We must cleanse this place. We must destroy his scent, his aura or bad things will come," Moses cried, almost hysterically.

James, attracted by the fuss, was a calming presence, as ever.

"Now come on, Moses. We all know that we left that particular nasty far behind. This is a very far way and we will not be destroying such an important site."

"But, Mister James, you do not understand. Where we were before was just one of his camps. Judging by these drawings, the beast lives here, or very close by."

"In the sacred elephant graveyard, ancestral resting place for the mightiest and most revered of beasts? I doubt that very much, my friend," James replied, with a benevolent smile.

But as he went to rest a reassuring hand on Moses' shoulder, he looked over and caught what looked like a faint glint appear in the torch-lit eyes of his wife. And if anyone knew the power of black magic, even in this desert, it was a third-generation daughter of a dark, sea wytch.

Yet, if there was anything familiar about this scene, Elouisa was giving nothing away. She stood impassively with their children, admiring the aura of this holy cave in such an important valley leading to a site of incredible spiritual power.

Given their experiences in the battle for the Black Castle, Holly was still more than a little wary of the darkness creeping back in. But while they were all together, the power of their connection seemed to sweep the looming doubts away.

Yet she was sure that fate had brought them to Africa for a reason. There must be a higher purpose, not just to ensure that Dinganwe, the leader of the elephants, fulfils his duties to those who had joined him here.

Meanwhile, out beyond the high canyon walls, moving relentlessly through the shadows, a presence most malignant drew closer every minute. It made its way toward its mistress, inching nearer to a long-awaited fate promised by the very stars that would be overlooking them all again that night.

At least three of their little gang may have sensed that something was amiss, but they certainly never spoke to each other about it. Perhaps they didn't want to jinx the excitement of this discovery for their father? Or perhaps it was because they were all a little scared?

Outside and high above, the sentinels on the hills saw nothing coming.

The animals gathered to pay tribute to the prince, felt nothing.

However, Moses knew that all was not well.

Henry's were-senses bristled with foreboding.

But only Elouisa, of all of them, felt a sense of mounting excitement that she couldn't quite put her finger on. It was a growing awareness of chaos, of delicious adventure, of change that was filling the dry air with the crackle of strange magic.

And for the first time during this trip, she started to feel Africa potently breathing magical life into the very skeleton of her old self again.

Like most demons and creatures of dark intent, the Tokoloshe is full of spite. It is more trickster than confronter, more sneak-thief than robber. It favours weasel words over roaring like a lion and when the demon comes for you, it is normally at night, while your guard is down.

But not today.

Today, it was so angry and excited and had been waiting for so long, that it made the creature almost foolhardy.

First, while the animal entourage was focused on their elephant prince and the passing ceremony, the evil imp crept through the long veld grass, all the way to the bank of the stream that bled from the waterfall and slipped into the crystal clear water.

As soon as the first, parched beast, a large, horn-crowned buffalo came to slake its thirst, the demon spilled its enchanted potion into the liquid the animal lapped, by urinating slyly into the water. Then, while its muzzle was numbed, the Tokoloshe slipped up the animal's large pink tongue and squeezed itself into his mouth.

From this very cramped position, it was able to operate the buffalo like a huge automaton or fleshy robot, walking slowly, and slightly dizzily, over to where a group of zebras stood transfixed, watching Dinganwe performing the ancient ritual.

They had all assembled here to pay their last respects to a much beloved member of their herd, who was crossing the bridge to immortality. It was a great privilege to witness a rite that all the animals held in the highest esteem.

In respectfully hushed tones, James was explaining the myths and legends surrounding the elephant's graveyard to his family and how this very ceremony had somehow featured in oral African folklore stories. Yet there were no accounts of any living person having witnessed it.

"It's amazing," whispered Alice, clearly in awe.

"We're so honoured to be here," agreed Holly, excited to the point of bursting, as their elephant friend worked his way through what were clearly some very important, symbolic gestures.

The assembled guests appeared to be humming, barely audibly and this created a sort of spiritual atmosphere with everyone focused on the same, pure thought.

Dinganwe was holding what appeared to be some sort of royal staff or rod in his trunk and at a particularly poignant moment, he used this to draw back a curtain of vegetation by the side of the waterfall.

This revealed another archway, framed by the largest elephant tusks imaginable, even larger than the ones they had passed through earlier.

Then slowly and solemnly, but purposefully, Dinganwe's elderly companion walked towards this ivory gate, passing from this earthly place to the next for the final time.

It was both a touching and an uplifting short journey for the assembled crowd, who looked on in reverential silence.

Yet while this ceremony was running its course, the demon had abandoned his temporary host, who had taken him to within feet of where the humans watched from the mouth of the cave. As it knelt, he slid from its throat, noiselessly.

It was so close now that the demon could almost smell its quarry. This was a worry, as it realised that if the wind changed direction, the lycanth changeling or were-creature boy would be able to smell it too.

So, the gremlin dropped quickly and drilled into the ground. It had chosen to lay in wait, like trapdoor spider. But it would bide its time and come out tonight, when the humans had succumbed to their greatest weakness, their need to sleep. And night was the Tokoloshe's domain.

The remainder of the ceremony of passing had been one of the most touching and respectful experience of the girls' lives. It almost matched the troubled reunion of their special family after a so much wasted time apart.

Once the curtains of vegetation had closed again, the animals began to file out solemnly and reverently. They each stopped to briefly honour and acknowledge their elephant prince, who waited patiently throughout.

When the last of the congregation walked through the archway, he nodded in the direction of their group and then made his way to a large, shaded area. Here he clearly set to rest.

Despite the skeletal company of the dead, Elouisa was most insistent that they camp in the mouth of the sacred cave. James was a little surprised but delighted at the chance for further study and soon set about photographing, drawing and documenting with a passion.

This left Moses and the children to sort out their accommodation and set up camp between them.

They were all too touched by the day's events to chat much

and just got on with the practical work of starting the campfire, prepping dinner, unrolling sleeping bags and erecting bug nets.

None of the adults felt the need to set a guard that night, given the animal sentinels they knew would be protecting the secret valley. So, after a quick and lazy game of "guess the astral constellation" while staring at the most amazing night sky of a billion twinkling lights, they were all soon sleeping soundly.

As threatened, around 2 a.m, the witching hour, something sinister stirred in the sand. Anyone with eyesight acute enough would have seen a series of small indentations making their stealthy way from the pool to where the family slept.

Sure enough, it was the Tokoloshe, who had earlier taken a long drink of water to become invisible and was tiptoeing over the last few yards.

The sinister night walker was relieved to see that the dog boy was near the back of the slumbering group.

The first person it came to was the father, closest to the cave mouth.

The monster was momentarily transfixed by the human's exposed throat and ran its mouth over his wet lips to taste the magic there. But it grimaced at the musky confirmation that it was not him it sought.

Tiptoeing round the man on its invisible pig-like trotters, it then paused at the next sleeping bag. This time it was the dark-haired girl.

It had no interest in the children, however, as the creature knew from their smell that they too tasted bad. The cloak she was using as a pillow, also gave it the jitters, for some reason. It was as if it was alive.

So, on it moved.

At the third sleeping bag it paused, as this one seemed to shift a little. But holding its raspy breath, it could sense it was not the quarry it came for. So, it waited until the moving stopped and then slipped past to its target.

There, at last, was she. The mother. The queen witch.

Trying hard not to wheeze with excitement, it soon came upon the sleeping place of Elouisa. Slowly, it crept toward where her face, her mouth should be. And then it unsheathed, in full this time, that surprisingly long and foul-smelling tongue, dabbing at the mouth of the bag, tasting, searching.

But it was disappointed to find nothing but down-filled sleeping sack. Then it was frozen by a sharp sudden sentence:

"Looking for something?" came a voice from the darkness, on a ledge in the cave, right above where it stood.

"Yes, I see you. Why so surprised, pig-demon?"

Her voice was calm but disarmingly steely and commanding.

It froze the creature to the spot.

Yet what happened next took place in a spark and a blur of activity.

First, a flash of lightning struck the ground where the demon stood. This soon stripped it of its best defence, its invisibility, and illuminated it from head to horns for all to see.

It spat out its scalded disgust and hissed its contempt.

Second, as the Tokoloshe coiled in its fury and leaped at Alice, who had cast the spell with the Willowand, its sharp teeth and clawing talons encountered nothing but a strong barrier force.

Holly had woken and, realising the danger, in a blink faster than a thought, had commanded the Rubyrobe to shield her sister.

The robe was impenetrable to the nasty little beast's worst assault and its repeated efforts simply blunted its sharp, filthy teeth and long yellow talons.

But the third and final ignominy came when it found itself lifted into the air by an invisible, pinching force and then slammed into a large clear, liquid-filled container.

"Ayeee," cried Moses, most delighted at having scruffed the beast.

"It is most fitting that I, from a long Nyanga line of holy men should capture you, dark crawler, daemon of the night."

He was doing a sort of happy jig on the spot as he spat out those words, such was his excitement.

"Behold your new nest, your water den where you shall rest at no risk to biting the toes from these fine people. We see you now, witch beast, we do see you now."

Their guide had placed the monster in a large glass jar that had been used to preserve some very delicious peaches they had eaten for supper. It had been filled with spring water and was now a unique tank or cage for the captive.

"We fooled you, daemon. You walked into our trap. And now you are mine."

At these words the Tokoloshe scraped its sharp tusks and then fangs down the glass in a desperate effort to break it. But to no avail. It was clearly incandescent with absolute rage at being outsmarted and fooled.

Elouisa, however, in the meantime, had climbed down faster than she usually moved.

She swept the jar from Moses' hands before he could react, snarled under her breath to silence him when he made as if to say something, and was now studying its contents very closely under her torch. She then reached into her jacket and took out a large, black book that had no business fitting into her pocket.

"Nicely spotted, Henry," said James, to break the tension surrounding what had just happened, placing a protective arm round his son. "None of us would have known the creature was here but for your excellent sixth sense."

His mother had now taken the jar nearer to the fire and was gazing at it enquiringly. The magnifying glass exaggerated the daemon's features markedly. She was gazing from creature, then back to the book like a professor in a museum with some sort of rare new specimen.

"I knew it would be here in the Book of the Dead," she cried triumphantly.

Strangely, the hideous critter had become calm, as if hypnotised by Elouisa's attentions.

Rather than thrash about, as it had, it appeared to fold its arms and legs and sink to the bottom as if dropping into a comfy armchair.

The creature's ease started to sow unease in the two men, who glanced over at each other with furrowed brows.

For, worse still, rather than struggle, it now had a grin spreading all over its ugly, pock-marked, wide face. It was a look best described as that of young love and this demeanour quickly spread from ear to hairy pig-like ear.

Lucy and Savannah were still puzzled by what had just happened to them in the sinister Mousehole cottage.

Things had not worked out as they had expected, not at all. And now they found themselves sitting down around a rustic kitchen table to a late afternoon cream tea.

"Remember to put the cream on afore the jam, girls," laughed Madame Rebecca heartily, "'tis the Cornish way tha knows!"

Both ladies seemed to be in their element in the presence of their creepy old friend, who, it turns out, was a Druid, one of the most ancient of magickal folk.

Suddenly all the plants growing everywhere, the animation of the shrubs in the doorway and the sage-like smell made perfect sense. For Druids, as they both knew, are powerful elementals who draw their skills from the things that grow and thrive in nature.

The raggedy ginger tomcat was now purring in the old man's musty lap, neither partaking of the tasty teatime treats on offer, Lucy noticed. This jogged her memory about something else the field mouse had mentioned to them and, typically, she couldn't keep the question in.

"Um…Brinn," she started, hesitantly.

He must have been able to hear the nerves in her voice, as he raised his eyes for the first time and peered at her from beneath his long, grey fringe. This made Lucy both more nervous and more determined to press on with her question.

"Do you have a basement?"

Savannah flashed a horrified look at her sister and couldn't believe she had just asked that question.

"That's a strange thing to ask, petal," NJ said, placing her hand on Lucy's shoulder as if to curtail any more embarrassing enquiries.

But she was cut short by their host who, first cleared his throat loudly and then in his cracked, tired voice, asked, "What is it to thee, child? What know you of this ancient place?"

Lucy was not one to be averted from her course once set upon it, as her family knew well. And as she went to reply she could see his eyes fixed upon the Ravenring, which was starting to tingle a little on her finger.

"Well, I couldn't but notice the green light around the skirting boards. Seems to suggest that there could…." Her voice trailed off as she saw him grimace a little as if found out.

"How very clever of one so small," he cackled, in an admiring if patronising tone of voice.

"But then, that would be my business now, wouldn't it? And not everything is children's business too, no matter how….special they thinks they may be."

He then paused, smiled a lopsided, wrinkly-faced smile at the ladies then added under his breath, "Despite what modern mums mights say."

The two ladies, feeling the tension rise, laughed nervously. By the looks they exchanged they were clearly wondering what was going on now?

He obviously did not know Lucy, however.

Rather than be browbeaten by the Druid, Lucy suddenly rose to her feet and, as if being led by her ring finger, walked up to one of the walls. Before anyone could say anything else, she then wiped her arm upward, tracing a rectangular shape which glowed bright green for a few seconds. Then, before several shocked jaws could close, a door magically appeared.

While the shocked throng was frozen, she then reached down and pulled on the handle.

In a split second, the room was alive with a cloud of hundreds of clicking, screeching and fluttering shapes. A veritable swarm of bats exploded among them and seemed to suck out the last of the dusty air as they raged.

"The door," Brinn cried, "Open the kitchen door!"

Savannah, who was closest, made for the door, but before she could get there, a pulsating power emanated from where Lucy had stood.

Looking up, she could see the bats now swarming around her sister. She was now just a blur of colour somewhere in the middle of the maelstrom.

A sort of green and black glow grew with each throbbing pulse and then the mob started to thin, and she could see that the bats were streaming, flowing into the Ravenring as if channelled by a compelling force.

The power of the ring was swallowing the swarm whole. It was some sight to behold.

Brinn, while this was happening, held his hands up as if to shield his eyes. He then backed away from the epicentre of the maelstrom, retreating to the shadows at the back of the room.

Perhaps not surprisingly, the ginger tomcat was nowhere to be seen.

JJ, however, was running around the room, hopping and leaping, snapping and trying to catch bats.

The strange phenomenon ended almost as soon as it had begun after the last of the bats had been sucked into the magical artefact.

In a few seconds, all that remained was three aghast adults, shocked at what they had just seen, two sisters dazed and confused, a couple of puzzled four-legged companions and a gaping door which appeared to be a portal to somewhere mysterious.

Where it led, however, was anybody's guess.

Yet typically, Lucy certainly couldn't wait to find out.

"I am absolutely mortified by your behaviour," said a clearly irate Nanna, as she marched the sisters back down the long lane.

"We were guests enjoying an old friend's hospitality and you billowed in like a sea storm of flying rats. What were you thinking?"

"To be fair to Lucy," offered Savannah, her usual calm and reassuring tones soothing the fraught scene, "Lucy and I were very worried about you both. We may have got a little carried away, but we thought you were in danger."

NJ walked on in silence for a few steps until Madame Rebecca breezed into the conversation, her usual vivaciousness breaking the tension as she laughed.

"Well, on the bright side, it certainly blew the cobwebs from Brinn's dusty life. Never seen him move so fast than when he slammed that door shut." She chuckled. "Then when Lucy let the bats out of the ring all at once! Not sure he'll ever get that kitchen clean again. The noise. And what a smell!"

NJ stared at her with a grumpy face at first, but as they all gradually burst out laughing, one after the other like a Mexican wave, she eventually caught the laughing bug too and chuckled.

"That poor old pussycat. It flew upstairs faster than a goblin on a gold coin. I thought JJ was going to have it for dinner at one point."

"I'm sure he will forgive us if we take him more cake and beer…. Eventually," laughed Rebecca, dabbing her eyes wet from laughing with a perfumed silk scarf.

Back at the cottage, however, things were not so jovial. While the Mousehole visitors boarded the Porthleven bus, the old Druid had been taking stock of everything he had just seen and experienced.

It had been a very many long years since such potent magic had surfaced on these shores.

The sight of the Ravenring and the aura conveyed by the young girls had awoken memories and feelings long suppressed.

With the full moon pending, the time had come to consult the elders. And that meant one thing. It meant a trip to visit the ancient seer, in the dank home of the decrepit crone.

So, reluctantly throwing his pale cloak about his slouched shoulders, he reached for his oaken staff. Then the ginger cat climbed his arm, still shivering slightly with shock.

"Come now, old grey-whiskered friend," he said, settling him on his neck while the creature complained in yowls and growls.

"I know. I hate it there too. But we have been putting this day off for far too long. Now we have little choice.

"If we do nothing, then all will soon be lost."

And with that, he carefully opened the concealed door again, less dramatically this time, mumbled a few words and illuminated his staff. Then they began the steady descent down the long, damp tunnel of tears.

The shivering of his familiar, his cat, did little to soothe him, For the feline's fears reflected his own feelings of terrible trepidation as well as his growing doubts about this unforeseen but doubtless fateful trip.

When the dolphins reunited to share the worrying news, the twins had been enjoying an energetic game of tag with a large school of mackerel.

Rainbow torpedoes daubed the sea with flashes of colour, like a sub-aqua firework display as the dolphins startled and scattered them.

Their sister's hasty return, worried manner and worrying news, however, punctured their fun bubble.

But as they started to process what she was telling them about the deformed creatures by the Firehills, they all started to notice that the mackerel school had disappeared.

In fact, looking at their underwater domain, it seemed that every creature had swum, scuttled and squirmed into seaweed, sand or shell to get out of sight.

It was suddenly eerie and cold and deserted.

The dolphins instinctively formed a defensive triangle. They then sent out a warning signal to any of their extended pod who may be near enough to hear.

Dolphin language can be discerned for many sub-aqua miles and the amplification from three linked streams of sound meant their signal travelled fast.

With a trio of acute eyes scanning the seabed, they eventually spotted the spectre appear suddenly in their midst.

Seemingly swept in on an underwater wave of cold water, a creature that looked like two tiger sharks fused together in a macabre mash, swam chillingly between a clutch of granite rocks.

The late afternoon sunlight glinted on its shining, armoured skin lighting up a terrifying set of ragged, razor teeth.

It was scything its head from side to side as if in pain, clearly tasting the ocean, trying to track down something tasty. Then suddenly it stopped for a second. It pointed its sharp double-snout right at them, chilling the blood.

The attack came harder and faster than expected, skittling the dolphin crew.

It was soon clear that the beast was swift and aggressive but not the brightest as, rather than focus on one, it wasted a great deal of energy by chasing all three, chopping and changing as they darted and distracted.

Every time it singled out one of the mercurial dolphins, the other two hit hard with their tough beaks. They also tore chunks from one of its seven fins. Before long, the water was littered with sparkling shark bits. But what worried them was that it seemed to feel no pain at all.

Grace, who knew the shark tongue as she considered a visiting basking shark a great friend, tried reasoning with the beast. But despite several appeals to its good sense, while evading its aggressive lunges, the toothy monster showed no sign of understanding. It also showed no sign of growing tired or slowing down. Instead, it displayed another shocking burst of speed and caught the pacifying dolphin by her elegant tail until she shrieked in agonising pain.

The other two dolphins combined well to tease, torment and distract the shark-beast. They twisted, jumped and dove desperately above, beneath and beside it, weaving in and out of the sea weeds and kelp forest.

But unlike sharks they had fought before, this one seemed oblivious to their bunts as if it had no feelings. It held firm on their sister and even started to read their moves.

Eventually, however, in the face of a relentless battering and bruising assault, it released the dolphin who sank worryingly to the ocean floor. It then changed the pattern of its lunges and twisted its huge frame counter-clockwise until it caught the other twin off guard.

The blow from the gigantic double-head was like nothing the dolphin had ever felt before. The pain struck with an explosion of hurt. As teeth cut through his hide, he felt numb and could sense himself blacking out. Within seconds, he went limp and also started sinking as his sister had, completely at the mercy of their frenzied attacker.

Serena panicked. She battered their opponent relentlessly, like a jackhammer. But, undeterred, it now locked on the prone body of their brother and advanced, slowly but steadily, mouth agape.

Yet just as it seemed that Robby's fate was sealed as well, the huge, grey beast stopped, released him, then strangely, it started to spin.

The eldest dolphin instinctively put some distance between herself and the shark, swimming down to the now fallen twins.

While she did what she could to tend the wounded, who were turning the water cloudy with blood, the wereshark seemed to be at the core of an underwater whirlpool. It was revolving, round and round at an increasingly rapid rate, trapping the bizarre beast in a deep cone of water. The shark clearly had no way of breaking free from the watery cage.

Then the area lit up, as if the full face of the low sun had just appeared from behind a cloud, a warmth driving away the suffocating blanket of chilling dread that had accompanied their foe.

"Are you all ok?" asked a calm, nurturing voice they all knew well, projecting perfect Dolphin into their heads.

Then suddenly, swimming among them, her long blonde hair flowing and glorious trunk glistening green and deep blue down to the tip of her glorious tail, was Savannah. Her Moonstone necklace throbbed with the power it was taking to create the ocean vortex.

She had heard the dolphin's call from as far away as the beach at Porthleven. It had then taken just a few minutes to power swim round the headlands and bays.

Having dealt with the snaggle toothed terror, Savannah set about using her healing powers to tend to their badly battered, fallen friends.

She did what she could, but it was clear that she would have to treat the injured dolphins back at her cave and let the restorative waters work their wonder.

She only hoped that they weren't too late as, while Robby was complaining loudly, Grace no longer seemed to be moving much at all.

It was the ever-chattering vervet monkey colony that first spotted the poachers on the horizon, from the tips of the tallest trees.

Alerting the sentinels, it didn't take long for the message to filter down to the elephant prince who then called an emergency counsel of elders.

James and Moses were honoured to be included, while at the back of the cave Elouisa continued her intense, microscopic study of the captive demon.

The girls, meanwhile, busied themselves recording images of the incredible ancient artwork on their phones and then mingling with the animals yet to journey back from the sacred spot.

"We are worried that they will attack those who are soon to leave. And we are even more concerned that they will find our holy bestial place of reincarnation. For they come for our bones and for our tusks. If they find us here, we will be lost forever and our path to eternity will be shut off as many, many more of the dark humans will come."

The other animals nodded sagely as he spoke of their dilemma.

"Even with such depleted numbers, great Lord, we can still take them down," growled a large maned lion, with a great scar running down one side. He was clearly much respected by the assembled throng.

"But surely our losses will be great?" chattered a skittish zebra, voicing what many felt.

"Yes, they do have the death sticks that are faster than even the cheetah. Many of my people have fallen victim to their weapons." This quiet offering came from a grey bush rabbit who was stroking her chin with a white paw.

Dinganwe paused, listening carefully to all viewpoints.

"If I may make a suggestion," James stepped forward, so he could be more easily seen.

None of the animals thought to wonder how he could speak their language, for one of the magical effects of the spiritual valley that cradled them was that it restored ancient relations to how they once were, back before the time people and animal speak became confused, back to the time when people-kind sprung from the Onecave.

"If the remaining mourners exit to the south, beyond where the sun sleeps, we can double-back and ensure that the poachers never find their way here."

He had their attention but could feel the nervousness that centuries of poor relations between people and animals had engendered.

"We have already created traps and puzzles for them to cover our tracks. I can only imagine that the demon Tokoloshe somehow led them part of the way here, despite our efforts. But we can head them off, I can assure you."

A few of the animals sniggered at this bold statement, for, you see, they didn't understand, nor had they seen changelings before. And their experience of humans to date had not been favourable.

But the fact that Dinganwe simply turned his great head to one side to signal listening, soon silenced the doubters.

"Ah, yes, my friend. I have seen what you and indeed, your family can do. But these are very bad people. The stakes are high so you must be sure."

James smiled reassuringly. This frightened Moses who, to be frank, would sooner not be there at all.

"Yes, I have confidence in us. In my family. We shall hatch a plan and head out at first light. It will take them at least another couple of long days to plough through the deepest sand. We shall ensure that the sea of sand, and its many denizens, goes there to meet them instead."

"It is true that sometimes the greatest allies are the smallest," nodded the mighty elephant.

And with that, the gathering was brought to a close and James and Moses walked back to the cave.

"He is right, you know. Those are very bad people, and the omens are not good."

"Why?" asked James, smiling reassuringly but still puzzled and amused by his skittish friend.

"Tonight, there will be a red moon, the sign of death and

passing."

"Well, as much as I respect your beliefs, Moses, I am sure those omens apply to those evil people more than to us with hearts filled with kindness. Believe me, we have many surprises in store for them, some wretched shocks indeed. This very special place is too important to lose to evil people and their greed. I am sure you agree."

Moses nodded and smiled indulgently. But deep inside, his doubts fluttered like bird moths around a bright camp candle, destined to dance themselves to death.

Elouisa had been researching this spell for much of the night. She had not worked with these animals before so had to adapt the recipe from The Book of the Dead. But the sanctity of the sacred cave had increased her powers, and the summoning spell had proven to be far more potent than any she had cast before.

Scorpions, if you have considered closely, are like land crabs from the front, but with a startling sting in the tail, especially the little ones. They make up for punch with deadly potency. Most scorpions are not much larger than a beetle. But imagine thousands of them wriggling from the sand and creeping relentlessly toward you.

Well, that was what the poachers saw as they crested the sand dune. At first, they thought it a heat-haze, or a mirage of shimmering sands. But then they realised the truth. A sea of scorpions was flow-marching toward their slow-moving vehicle like a huge, shuffling carpet.

And it wasn't just the armoured insects that were on the move. For slithering by their side arose hundreds of deadly sand snakes.

Both sets of fresh horrors had a common destination or target in mind. And as they rippled across the red sand, it now looked like the very earth was alive.

Guns were, of course, no good to the gangsters now. But they fired off rounds into the sand, regardless in a desperate attempt to fend off this latest plague. Wide-eyed and terrified, they all crammed into the small cabs, locked all the doors and barricaded all the windows.

Soon, the inside of their battered bakkies were like ovens, with all the bodies crammed in on such a hot desert day. The scorpions were crawling over every inch of the caravan of cars, causing the blinded drivers to grind to a halt.

Commanding the power of the elements, James then summoned the wind again to re-shape the dunes.

The sand vibrated and shifted beneath the cars, revolving them through 180 degrees until they were facing completely the opposite direction. Then, with a wave of his arm, he launched the bakkies full of poachers on the craziest sand magic carpet ride, propelling them back and out of sight.

"I shan't imagine we shall see them again," his wife laughed as she looked on, impressed by her husband's more elemental powers, and clearly enjoying the chance to stretch her own magical legs.

"And just as well," said Holly, a little frustrated that they hadn't managed to do much. "Hopefully the secret of the elephant's graveyard will be properly safe now."

But as they prepared to return, Henry's nose started twitching once more.

He stopped and scanned the horizon.

"What is it, H?" asked Alice, more attuned to her brother's ways.

He didn't have time to answer, however, before they were surrounded by the cloying stench of a mob of hunchbacked terrors.

Taking advantage of the distraction, the hyena pack had returned.

And at its head was a beast four times the size of any of the others, walking on its hind legs.

Henry's heart sank when he recognised the creature he had fought with, that night at their camp. It was transformed now to many times its previous size, and by the look of its drooling jaw, several times as mean.

It dawned on Henry and the adults that his own bite must have infected the predator with the lycanthrope virus. It had clearly invaded and colonised its blood, turning it rapidly into some sort of African hyena werebeast hybrid. And it was now hell bent on revenge for the indignity suffered.

Either boosted by their leader's presence or bullied by him, the mob were strangely courageous and were closing fast on all sides.

James and Elouisa joined hands and started an instinctive incantation, moving their conjoined arms in a circular motion until a perimeter of purple light erupted around them. This created a magical force field impenetrable to most acts of nature.

"That should hold them," James shouted above the snickering and whooping and snarling noises.

However, their plan had one rather major fault. For the lead beast was no longer simply a force of nature. It now had were-magic flowing through its body and judging by its demeanour, it was starting to realise the power this bestowed upon it.

"Deet you theenk yor seely lights would protec you, priddy girls?" he slavered, terrifyingly, before uttering a bone-chilling roar.

Then he leaped.

He came on so fast down the dune, that they had only split seconds to react. That was just enough for both Holly and Alice to burst from human to faerie form, leaving the crazed animal snapping at empty air and sharp sparkles.

Holly was the first to counter and out of nowhere conjured a long line of scarlet stars in a looping chain, which she deftly cast around the neck and muzzle of the snapping beast. Next, with surprising strength, she drew it tight and brought the mangy creature to its knees.

Then, with the Willowand, Alice created a football-sized glowing ball of energy. With a waft of her hand, she used this as a bludgeon to knock the snarling abomination back beyond the ring of protection, like a tennis player hitting a forehand smash into an opponent at the net.

While her children fought, their mother took something from a pouch in a trouser pocket and added the potion to the magical current. This made it transform from purple to sable black, humming with power.

Although liberated from its restraints, it was clear the hybrid hyena did not feel able to re-cross the threshold. It had tasted the combined force of the family and it had no appetite for more.

However, the snapping pack, ravenous with hunger and angered by the setback, only retreated a short distance before settling down to wait. They clearly intending to lay siege and to tease them out.

"This creature, my people call Porlo the Nandi, or the Nandi Bear. For that must be what it is," said Moses, feverishly. It is most evil and will surely feast upon our bones if..." he then realised that, despite their changeling powers, he was still potentially frightening children. So he stuttered to a clipped halt.

Moses looked to the horizon instead, where night was about to fall like a stage curtain, ushering in the red moon.

"Eish! The Nandi becomes stronger in the night. So, we must make a plan and act soon, my friends, or we are surely lost."

James nodded in acknowledgement and Elouisa rubbed her characteristically large forehead as if trying to inspire a plan.

Then after a few minutes of silence she announced, "I have an interesting idea."

She paused.

"But, I'm afraid you're really not going to like it."

The children and Moses tried to distract themselves by chatting in a sort of square, with their backs to the adults who were now having a full-scale row. It had started when their mother had informed him of her plan, in private.

Despite their efforts to block them out, what she had in mind seemed...crazy.

"There are too many of them now. Must be a hundred or more and they are not going to be contained by the shield for much longer. It is draining me faster because there is very little here to sustain it, James."

Their body language was very revealing. Mother was in full flow while Pops was wringing his hands and pacing.

"But you just don't know what it is going to do, Leez. You must consider the risks to the children. Let me...."

"What?" she retorted. "Martyr yourself again, like....?"

He looked up.

"Like last time, when you...." but his words petered out as he realised they would not return to his mouth should he spill them.

"Ah! So now we see the truth," Elouisa replied, slowly. "You are still holding a grudge about Berkhamsted Castle. You…."

"Enough!" he replied, cutting off the too familiar tit-for-tat refrain. "Enough!"

He tried to look into her eyes, but she turned her cheek in anger, averting her gaze.

"No, I do not, and I am sorry that I raised it."

"AGAIN!" she snorted. "Raised it yet again…"

"Again," he replied, sadly, knowing he had just surrendered any counter argument he could make.

"So, it is decided then," she announced suddenly, changing moods like gears on a car, and walked over to the back of their vehicle, stepping outside the circle to do so by facing down the pairs of eyes watching her from the shadows.

Even hungry hyenas would surely fear her, glowing wand drawn, in this frame of mind.

From the rear of the vehicle, she removed an object covered in a dark sheet and then returned to the protected place, to focus on the job now at hand.

Nobody else could really see what Elouisa was up to, as it was quite dark now.

So, they busied themselves, sorting out a fire using wood they brought with them and oil torches on long stems.

While they were doing this, Alice looked over and could see her mother mumbling what was clearly some form of incantation. Light was reflecting back onto her face, bouncing off what she was sitting in front of, cross-legged on the floor in a repose, like something else she had seen recently.

"The Tokoloshe," she uttered out loud, inadvertently. "She's talking to the Tokoloshe."

This froze the others to the spot, as they looked over nervously and saw her, slowly unscrewing the lid, her chanting voice rising as she did.

Moses made as if to object. But it was too late. For now, the snuffling, pig-beast clambered from its watery confines, like a slimy cork from a bottle and dropped to the floor, breaking wind loudly as it landed.

"Sies!" exclaimed Moses. "Grab it, you madwoman, or it will surely kill us all."

Before anyone could react, however, it stuck a long middle finger up at them. Then it inserted the digit into a dribbling nostril with a sigh. Eventually it pulled out a sizeable goblet of yellow snot, popped this into its mouth and disappeared, vanishing without so much as a puff of smoke.

Moses was most animated now and couldn't suppress his exasperation at what had just occurred.

"No, no, no, no," he repeated, beating his forehead with the palm of his hand.

Henry, however, simply shook Holly by the shoulder and pointed at the sand.

"Look!"

Trotter-sized footprints were now heading straight for the largest of the dunes. This was also where the bulk of the scavengers were waiting.

The prints paused at the perimeter of the magic-circle while

Elouisa cast a gateway charm to allow it passage. Then she sealed it again shortly thereafter.

Nothing happened for a good minute or so.

Then out of the blue, they heard an almighty, ear-splitting yelp from the brow of the dune.

All hell broke loose suddenly as something seemed to set the hyenas on each other.

First, one flew through the air, knocking a group of four over like standing dominoes. They then attacked each other, drawing others into the brawl, teeth flashing and large jaws snapping.

About half the assembled force of representatives from what must have been a dozen packs was soon fighting amongst themselves. Saliva and snapping teeth filled the sky. For a truce amongst highly territorial scavengers is only ever paper thin.

Just as they thought things couldn't get any more chaotic, the leader tumbled down the dune, clearly clutching at its hind leg. It was oozing blood where something had assaulted it.

Instinct took hold of Henry, and having transformed in a few seconds, he too was quickly racing toward the now-vulnerable Nandi hyena in his alternative form.

The moon glistened on his dark and silver fur, accentuating his sleek mane and his juvenile muscles.

Henry was not so large as his foe, but he was young, keen fit and fast and strong. He also had surprise on his side, as the hyena leader was still clutching at its leg as if trying hard to shake something off.

The other hyenas scattered and ran as he arrived. He dove onto the monster and grappled it from behind, establishing a headlock intended to subdue and restrain.

But he underestimated its power. It howled like something caught in the jaws of a metal trap then shook itself free of both his grip and the assailant on its leg.

The two lycanths now faced each other, slowly circling to their right as they searched for an opening. Other than a marked limp, the monster seemed remarkably well, which was troubling.

"Soooo, I have you all to miyself, leetle puppeee!"

It snarled the words more than spoke them.

"I tasted yor flesh befor. Now I feeenish yew."

But, interestingly, it did not rush at him as expected, causing Henry to suspect that the damage it sustained from the Tokoloshe was worse than first imagined, causing it to bluff.

Then he remembered something Moses had said about them having venom on their teeth, and he gazed into the beast's eyes for signs of the spread of the poison.

While they snarled at each other, the Tokoloshe was now causing carnage amongst the rest of the gang. Yelps were ringing round the mob as here a tail was bitten, there some toes taken or a flank was slashed by a tusk. Soon many started to flee the menace in the darkness.

What he couldn't see, however, was that the magical force field had de-activated and his family were in a desperate struggle with what must have been about twenty or so hungry hyenas that had ambushed them from the dark rear.

A group of vultures also appeared to have joined the fight; unusual for carrion crawlers who normally only came for the casualties, the dying and the dead.

Moses was giving a good account of himself with a large, wooden club or knobkerrie. It seemed to be more powerful than it should be, as he scythed through the flying nasties until the air was alive with feathers.

Holly and Alice were zipping around between the torches, sending animals skyward as they worked their magic. And James was plucking the flying furies from the skies, diverting the power of the wind and air to knock the flocks of vultures to earth.

Elouisa, however, unbeknown to the others, was struggling. Retaining the protective circle, and her work with controlling the Tokoloshe, had clearly drained her and she was only just about holding three of the more persistent beasts at bay. She was, though, slowly but surely being driven back toward the car.

As she drew closer to the vehicle and the promise of some shelter, to her horror, another snickering animal appeared and cut off her escape route. She was now exhausted, and she was surrounded.

When her assailants slavered and growled, she hissed and spat back at them like a feral cat, hurling curses and incantations. She countered every lunge they made with a hand gesture of her own that blocked a snout or shut their fetid mouths with small bursts of magic energy. But as fast as she did this, the next attack came. Then the next. Then the next. Until inevitably she felt her knees start to buckle.

To cap it all, the witch was making her last stand tucked to the rear of the car where her family couldn't see. She tried to edge back into the light of the torches but each time she moved, the carnivores countered by sliding across.

Elouisa could feel herself growing dizzy. She now started to hyperventilate through her mouth. She was panicking because she knew what was coming next.

Extreme magic fatigue is a very serious malady for magic users. And her energy levels were now so dangerously low. To maintain the power, the magic was starting to feed on her soul.

Inevitably, it happened. She started to slip into unconsciousness. And as the black veil fell, the last thing she was aware of was the rotten stench of the hot breath and the spittle of several of the beasts on her face.

Meanwhile, up on the hill, Henry was not faring much better.

He was now seriously doubting his ability to take down this creature of his own creation by himself. He feared he was just that touch too inexperienced against such a wily foe and he was now regretting his rashness and arrogance.

Self-doubt can be a crippling thing, but he steeled himself, despite himself, thought brave thoughts and focused.

"Kam on, furry boy," mocked his opponent. "I am going to enjoy crushing your bones to the marrow."

He was too busy insulting Henry in a leering voice, however, to notice that a very pretty, dark-haired girl had softly landed behind him.

She appeared to be holding a tyre lever, or something similar. The next time he opened his huge mouth to hurl more vile abuse, the girl brought the lever down on its muzzle with as much force as she could muster.

As the creature choked back a howl of pain, she took two steps to the side and spread the red robe before her. It was now difficult to see where her body was positioned.

When the animal ran at her, as she knew it would, she deftly flicked the robe to one side like a matador or bull fighter. She then launched herself noiselessly into the air in the same movement, like a swimmer pushing away from the side of the pool at pace.

Both children watched from above as the beast tumbled over the steep edge of the cliff. It was screaming with anger and frustration as it plummeted, presumably to a sticky end, as they imagined even werehyenas don't bounce too well.

Henry thought for a few seconds that he might give chase, just to be sure. But his urge to proud-hug Holly was stronger.

Their delight at the tumble of the toothy terror, however, was cut short by the noise from below.

James, covered in mess and fur was roaring in anger and anguish as he ran towards where his wife had fallen. As he ran, he could only watch in horror as she was set upon by at least four of the hyenas. One had taken her by the back and was shaking her limp body.

Moses too looked on desperately from further back, dispatching another of the animals with a backhanded swipe. His heart sank. But what he saw next defied belief.

Just as it seemed as though the hungry animals would tear the witch apart, fur started to fly. Something unseen was tearing into them. It was like somebody was attacking them with huge garden shears, hacking off mangy mane in clumps. And they were understandably terrified.

After a few seconds of this frenzied invisible assault, all four hyenas turned and ran, some losing more chunks of fur and flesh as they did. An ear fell to the sand. One sorry beast that didn't tuck its tail between its legs fast enough quickly found itself with nothing but a stump.

Then, bar a few bodies, in seconds all their foes were gone and silence descended.

As James reached his unconscious wife, his attention was caught by the sudden appearance of an odd figure.

The Tokoloshe materialised from nowhere. And it was munching, rakishly on a hyena tail like it was a long, hairy sausage. Most disturbingly, it was also grinning proudly as it chewed.

Savannah, back on the Cornish coast, decided to carry out her own investigations of the underwater Firehills, after hearing the full extent of the dolphins' tales while they recovered from their injuries in her crystal pool.

She was shocked by what she found.

Clearly something was leaking into the ocean through those bubbling, gaseous outlets and it was having a very damaging effect on the sealife in the area.

"But that bizarre shark, in these cool waters?" she thought, mortified.

Now that was a new and a very disturbing development for all of them, especially as they were coming into prime season for holidaymakers. And the water was, of course, one of the main attractions in these parts.

Rather than rush back to their cottage in Porthleven or stop off at the crystal cave, her home for so many of the lonely years, she decided that some exercise was needed to clear her mind.

Making sure that they swam undetected until away from the main coastal paths and beaches, she raced the now healed dolphins underwater at first.

She was pleased to see that she was still faster than them under the surface, so decided to push herself.

First, she pressed the Moonstone, ensuring that she was cloaked in the shimmering invisibility this gave her while in water. Then she burst the surface and alternated racing dives with the dolphins.

However, they were like flesh missiles and incredibly acrobatic, excelling at this sport. Soon they had rushed ahead and left her behind, so caught up were they in their competitive games, full of fresh vigour from the healing waters.

So, Savannah decided to pay a trip to one of her favourite spots instead. It was the beautiful Kynance Cove, or Gwyrdh Mogow, as she called it, after the ancient Cornish language that is so like mermaid speech.

Kynance was a very popular place with holidaymakers who delighted in its beautiful beaches and very many grottos, caves and inlets that changed by the minute with each variation of the tide or wind.

In fact, she had heard a group of special, thrill-seeking children once call a section of the rocks that created a tunnel, channelling the incoming water, the washing machine or womb of doom, presumably describing the impact of the onrushing sea on their splashing, bathing bodies.

Regardless of how busy it was, there were special caves that were only accessible from the seaward side. Yet because of the guardian rocks and sharp-rising cliffs, only an expert seaman could navigate into there without considerable jeopardy.

She, of course, had no such problems. But it did amuse and thrill her to be gliding through the water literally feet away from families leaping and cavorting in the waves, baking in the sand or searching for treasure in the many rock pools.

All were oblivious of her. She had long become accustomed to the unseeing of adult humans. They had stopped believing so had stopped seeing the magic that abounds in everyday life. Although ever so occasionally, a particularly perceptive young child with a stronger sense of faith in magical creatures might just catch a glimpse of something glistening in the green sea and know instinctively she was there, only to be sadly "poo-pooed" by an adult or their cynical friends.

In the blink of an eye, Savannah was walking into the beautiful jade, ruby and gold serpentine cavern, wet, wild and always wonderful.

Today she shared her special place with a couple of sun-bathing crabs and a rainbow-beaked puffin, clearly taking a rest from harvesting silver sand eels from the garden on the seabed.

"Hello," smiled the mermaid, as warmly as is her want.

"Oh," grumbled the puffin, a bit grumpily. "I was having a

snooze."

She chuckled at his brooding, clown-like face thinking how much people love these adorable birds, as capable under water as they are flying. No wonder they were knows as this coast's penguins.

"Well I'm sorry to disturb you. But I was wondering whether you had seen old Goelann?"

"That smelly old seagull? The one who chases the choughs away and tries to snatch our eggs every breed season or pinch our catch? Well, yes, as it happens, he's up there on the ledge outside, catching the afternoon sun, I imagine before setting off on another of his wretched raids. A feathered pirate that one, I tell ya."

Savannah thanked the moody fellow and wandered in the direction he had sent her, down a small passage connecting this cave to the next.

The serpentine rock and granite had been hollowed out because of millions of years of relentless action from the waves. But given how hard it is, it always amazed her how powerful nature can be.

As she gripped an overhanging ledge to wriggle round the bend in the tunnel, the stone gave way in her hand, causing her to lose her balance.

"That battle with the shark must have taken more out of me than I thought," she mused.

She swung round the rock face with rather less agility than she showed in the water, her natural domain. This time she slipped and landed square on her bum, knocking some of the wind from her lungills.

Luckily, however, the grumpy puffin had nodded straight back off to sleep, so he missed her fall, sparing her blushes.

As she put her hands down to push herself back up, something about the rock that had come away in her hand caught her eye.

"Did that just flash?" she said out loud, without realising.

"Fish?" came an irritated voice from just outside the cave. "Did somebody say they have fish?"

Suddenly, in a scrum of white-grey feathers, gangly wings like elbows and exuding the strong smell of diesel and week-old seaweed, appeared Goelann, probably the oldest seagull in Cornwall, if not the world, as he often reminded people.

"Oh!" he cried, as he saw Savannah. "What are you bloomin well doing here? We all thought you'd returned to Grockle land. You know? Grown back your legs and given up your tail......Oh! I see you have," he said, a bit rudely, pointing at her legs with a flappy, tatty wing. "What an ugly lump that is at the end of your back."

"Nice to see you too, Goelann," she laughed, rubbing her buttocks as she did, stone still in hand.

"What's that you've got there?" he asked. "Doesn't look much like dinner to me. And I missed breakfast too," he grumbled.

"Tell the truth, I'm not too sure. Just thought it was a loose bit of serpentine rock but...."

Just then the sun stretched its arm and long fingers into the mouth of the cave where they were standing. To their surprise, as soon as the light caressed the stone, something very special happened. Suddenly things started falling from it. Crusted-on stone and grit and barnacles started crumbling to the floor, dissolving like a sandcastle's walls when the tide rushes back in.

Then, when Savannah took it to the mouth of the cave and washed it in the sea water, something truly fascinating emerged. She turned to the old seagull and held aloft a very beautiful green stone short dagger or blade.

"Heavens above, and the ancient blue and green gods of the sea and skies, preserve us. For I do declare, Missy Mermaid, that what we both behold as sure as day is day and night is black, is nothing less than........"

"What?" she blurted, uncharacteristically.

"Well, it's only the legendary Jade Athame."

The coombs and crags of Kynance Cove had kept this secret to themselves for what must have been centuries.

An athame is a very potent magick item in the mystical art of Pagans, Wiccans or ancient magick users. Athames of various shapes and sizes feature in the Witchcraft Museum in Boscastle. And this appeared to be an extremely special example, far better than any the mermaid had ever seen.

"Most older types from these parts know the ancient sea shanty sung by the fisher folk from Port Isaac down to the aged shores of Gweek.

"One tells the tale of a wretched sea crone.

I used to hang around the dock bars down the hill at Port Isaac waiting for chips n pasties and would often hear the drunken sailors sing of her. Me memory is going a bit but as I recall, her song goes a bit like this."

The seagull cleared his throat forcibly, coughed up a fish bone, then sang in a voice like someone gargling with ground sea glass during a storm.

"For twenty score years
She lived by the river.
For twenty score years
She lived by the sea.
A foul crone she was
Our souls she was cravin'
With her great Jade Athame
Our livers stole she.
Oh I......"

He suddenly started coughing, waving his wings as he spluttered.

"Darn it...I've forgotten how the rest goes now. Not the same when you haven't been gobblin' pasty crusts n batter and sipping beer dregs, mine-sweeping from left glasses."

Savannah smiled and ran her hand down the back of his long neck, leaving a sort of soothing warmness in its wake.

"There, there," she sighed. That was a very...entertaining rendition. You have a voice of great....character."

If it's possible for a seagull to smile, this one did.

"But what does it mean?"

"Well...apparently she was a sea wytch who tormented these parts, snatching children and their pets and that kind of thing. Some say she used to eat 'em. Others say she kept 'em captive to do her foul bidding coz nobody would marry such a terrible hag. And THAT, m'lovely, by my reckoning, was the magic dagger she used in her rituals, to stir her cauldron, to land her spells."

Savannah suddenly felt a strange sensation come over her and she dropped the object with a start, like it was a live coal.

"What's the matter?"

"It moved. I swear it just moved in my hand."

"Don't be silly," said the old bird, waddling over to the dagger and examining it closely on the floor.

"Mmmm! Does seem to be glowing a bit, I must say."

"I am telling you. It moved. Like it was nuzzling my palm. Like a sand eel. It was creepy. Really creepy."

"I imagine, like all magical keystones and artefacts," he was looking at her necklace now, which was also glowing, "it needs a master or mistress. So, it was probably just bonding with you. Reading your soul. You know how that is," he nodded at the Moonstone.

"Of course. But like best friends. While we can hang around with others, we only ever really have one true bestie and I've found mine."

The sea horse and dolphin on the Moonstone necklace twinkled reassuringly as she spoke.

And with that, Savannah picked the green glass dagger up very tentatively. She then gingerly popped it into the chagrin purse she used to collect the sea treasures she kept in her undersea horde near the crystal cave.

Then, with a "see you soon" to Goelann, she walked gracefully back into the sea.

Savannah barely caused a ripple as she swam out to the open water. As ever, she left no sign to betray that she had been there, other than some light footprints that could have belonged to any of the many holidaymakers laughing and giggling just a few feet away. But if you happened to be looking from above, you would have seen something glowing under the water as she sped, in her excitement, to find her sister and to share the latest news. But you would still, to this day, be debating what that underwater shape was.

Back south in the Namibian desert, the battle between the hyenas and the Savage throng had taken a terrible toll on the creatures of the night.

Unconscious bodies littered the dunes, some having limped or dragged themselves off into the darkness beyond the firelight.

Naturally, however, all the family currently concerned themselves with was the condition of their mother.

Her wounds had been tended. But she had slipped into a type of coma brought on by the exhaustion of her powers and whatever foul venom her cuts had ingested. She now needed complete rest.

"She should be fine, children," said their dad, not managing to completely conceal the concern on his face or in his voice.

With Elouisa secure and relatively comfortable in the back of the vehicle, all eyes now turned to what appeared to be her new familiar, or witch's companion.

"It is just sitting there," said Moses, barely able to conceal the repulsion in his voice.

The Tokoloshe was indeed perched on the roof of the car, directly above Elouisa, picking bits of hyena and Nandi out of its disgusting teeth with its own long toenails.

"Ugh, it repulses me," said Alice, sweeping her now rather sweaty locks from her face. "Look at the boogers running from its nose."

Henry, meanwhile, was growling, barely audibly. He clearly did not trust this demon, regardless of how it had helped her.

"Well. It did save Mom when none of us could get to her. So, it can't be all bad, can it?"

As ever, she tried to see the best in every situation and was a sucker for the underdog.

"We clearly can't camp here. It's too far back to the sacred valley, where we don't want to direct the poachers and we really can't travel far with Mom as she is. So, the plan is, we're going to head a few miles to the site of a spring Moses knows about. He thinks we should be able to set up camp relatively safely there as it's baboon territory and not a place where the predators venture."

So, Holly wrapped her mother in the Rubyrobe, which warmed her through with its healing powers. James drove, with the aid of the powerful safari spotlights mounted on the roof, and Moses directed, standing on the passenger seat, having peeled back part of the canvas roof.

None of them had been able to get the desert gremlin to move.

It sat on the roof as if glued to the spot, something Moses found extremely off-putting given his face was often just a few feet from those razor-sharp, diseased, toe-chomping teeth.

With the children curled up on each other in the back seat, dreaming of a fresh oasis at the end of a very long, hot and stressful day, this unique band of changeling adventurers made slow progress into and then through the starry, starry African night.

Book 3:
The Jade Athame

Behind him, hundreds of multi-coloured butterflies had started gathering around the entrance to the cave.

The pattern on their wings was like a thousand eyes, a peacock glinting in the beams of the sun.

They were clearly attracted to whatever was in the powder James had used.

But it was as if they too had crowded in to pay homage to the home of the ancient African queen.

Druids are ancient mystical folk with powers that come from nature itself. Their spiritual order was seemingly ended during the Roman occupation of Britain, supposedly because of their reputation for local leadership and for taking human sacrifices to increase their mystical strength. But despite the existence of many stone circles or henges and other Druidic places of worship throughout Cornwall, people, overall, are now completely unaware of the existence of Druid-kind. But they still walk among us today.

So the tired and cantankerous old man, Brinn had been easily able to go about his daily business all his life without anyone so much as batting an eyelid. Because, if truth be told, people often look but just don't see people, properly.

Most of us know that feeling, don't we?

It helped, of course, that the house that had been in his family since it was built had more than its share of clever secrets that few knew about.

As the old man and the ancient cat made their way down the secret tunnel, the Druid used his oak staff to sweep away the spider webs that seemed to have appeared every few metres since he had last been down here.

It was cold and damp and had an earthy smell. Roots from plants and trees had broken through in various places, doubtless providing homes to more than bats. It was a better den for a mole than a person.

Despite the lightness of his tread, his footsteps echoed off the stone walls and the shadows he cast loomed long and large.

He could feel the tension in the cat stretched around his neck and was conscious of his own breathing which, despite it being summer, appeared in mini vapour clouds before him.

After a steady plod that seemed to last for hours, they approached a large iron and wood door. It too was covered in dust and cobwebs, and toadstools grew about its base. Scuttling things seemed to cling to the various Wicca power pentangles and figures that were hung about it. Dreamcatchers and witch bundles, batches of sticks containing stones, skin and worse, tied with hair, were littered about the area.

These totems and power tokens were clearly to keep people out. But could they also be there to keep what lay beyond that ancient doorway in?

Rummaging in the long pocket of his faded and stained white robe, he fingered the large iron key, coldly clammy to his touch. With slightly trembling hands, he tried the huge lock, half hoping that it had rusted shut since his last visit.

But his heart sank when he heard the hauntingly familiar click of the mechanism sliding and the door unlocking, with what seemed like a tired sigh of resignation, a secret betrayed.

For the first time since they started their subterranean trek, Skibbers showed some enthusiasm. Or it may just have been that the old cat knew the routine and was resigned to what was going to happen next.

Before Brinn could pull the heavy door all the way open, he had slinked through the crack and disappeared inside without so much as a glance back.

"Well, charming," muttered the old man to himself. "Not so brave with the bats, but keen to see what mice have been making themselves at home in the fisherman's cabin, eh?"

Then as the door finally swung open, with a long groan like a dragon woken from a century of sleep, he raised his glowing staff.

Gradually, his magic light searched out and banished the shade from the dusty corners of the surprisingly large room. Then his eyes lighted upon the subject he dreaded but still sought.

There, seated at a low table in front of an unseasonal roaring fire, sat the slumped form of the giant. But before he could utter her name, she turned and looked at him.

This was something that the passage of time had never softened. Now staring back at him were those empty sockets that once were dark brown eyes. And they were screaming, in silence.

Elouisa was still in a deep magic-induced coma when they arrived at the oasis and started making camp.

As they put her to bed, James noticed, for the first time, a sort of yellowy, jaundiced hue to her skin and a fresh mole on her face.

He feared that this implied long-lasting after-effects of the poisoning pandemic of the Firehills mines back in their home county.

But he said nothing to the others.

Representatives of the baboon clan had been down at the natural well drawing water when the humans first appeared.

Moses and Henry had a brief, nervy meeting with the baboon elders. After exchanging some fruit, honey and oats they had remaining in their supplies, the larger males took up strategic positions around the camp while the nimbler in their number climbed the trees to keep watch.

But nobody really expected any more trouble, this night at least.

That evening, over another tasty safari meal, Moses regaled

them with stories of more amazing rock art by his ancestors, the San people in a place called Twyfelfontein.

Apparently, they were now only a few hours' drive away and it was one of the sights James really wanted to study and write about.

Elouisa had started to show some signs of recovery and much to everyone's relief was now sitting up and complaining of thirst.

So, after a brief family conference, they decided that their job with the poachers was done, for now; that it was impossible for them to find the hidden valley and they could afford to get back to the holiday they had come here for.

For the first time in a while they all woke up refreshed, sleeping soundly under the protection of the baboons.

So they packed, left the last of the fruit and said their goodbyes, setting off across the desert before the sun could show off its might.

The evocatively named Twyfelfontein was another ancient settlement and the rock art they had come here to see was at the far end of another long-dried out riverbed forming a valley, then a gulley. The route there was marked by something called the lion head rock, an outcrop that looked like a roaring African king.

Moses guided them to the spot of the carvings and paintings which were largely on flat rocks scattered about the site. Once again, most of the depictions were of giraffes, ostriches, antelope and the other animals native to the area, which the children took great glee in imagining in their full splendour.

James, on the other hand, was running his hand along the solid rock wall of the small canyon. Inexplicably, he was attracted to the sheltered spot.

"There is nothing up there, Mister James," Moses said with a smile in his voice. "The archaeologists have been all over this site for many years. These amazing drawings are thought to have been revealed by mini avalanches when the rock has shifted."

James, however, could feel something that didn't make sense. On a solid face of sandstone rock in a parched desert terrain, he was sure he could detect some sort of a draft. Air seemed to be coming from behind the rock itself.

Reaching into one of the pockets in his safari jacket, he took out a small black container. He placed some of the contents in the palm of his hand and then rubbed his palm over an area of the rock where he felt the draft. Then he stood back, raised his arms either side of him and chanted something nobody could quite hear, while turning his palms upward to the sun.

The group watched with fascination as his palms started to glow. Even in such an exposed place on a cloudless, roasting hot day, they could see an intense light in his hands. Then, as if holding mirrors, he directed the sunlight in his palms to the area of rock he had just been rubbing.

As the beams of light hit the powder on the rocks, they ignited it, like welding rods, but rather than sealing they exposed a seam that ran in a ragged oval. James then stepped forward and tapped the centre with his right palm and before their eyes, the top layer of the rock slid away.

"How?" gawked Moses, his mouth as wide as his eyes.

Elouisa smiled with an almost forgotten pride.

"His elementalism is very special, very special indeed."

175

The girls were the first to rush forward, incredibly excited by what they could see.

Purple rays of light flashed from what appeared to be a large grotto.

James had already stepped through the threshold but waited for the children before moving further in.

He was glad they entered together as nothing could have prepared them for the sight that greeted them.

Huge amethysts were the source of the sparkle, creating a crystal tunnel of purple haze the like of which had never before been seen, certainly not by northern eyes. On instinct, both Holly and Alice changed to faerie form in a flash and flew in to accompany their father further.

Alice used the Willowand to create the light they needed to progress through the tunnel, its magical beams reflecting off the crystals and creating the illusion of a giant kaleidoscope. The others followed them in, slowly, awe-struck, eyes thirsty to drink in a sight that had blessed nobody for many thousands of years.

It was Holly who came upon the w first.

Holly was fluttering on lace-thin wings to the back of the large oval space at the far end of the amethyst tunnel when the aura compelled her to go further.

There, carved from what appeared to be polished soapstone, mounted on a plinth at the centre of the room, was a figure clad in what they all now recognised as the traditional clothes of the San people, Moses's tribe.

She had a swollen belly, as if carrying a child, balanced by gracefully accentuated buttocks. She was life-size but somehow larger than life and she was breathtakingly beautiful.

But that wasn't what made her father and mother stop breathing.

As Alice lit up the whole of the room, they could also see a painting or etching that ran the length of the room. Incredibly, it depicted what any primary school child would recognise as a basic, but identifiable map of the continents of the world. Africa was twice the size of the others, but they were all there, all seven.

The painting seemed to show a group of people on a boat sailing the world's seas and oceans. Each continent contained carvings of some of the key creatures that make that continent unique.

They could clearly see kangaroos in Australia, buffalo in North America, a hippo in Africa and an Asian bear.

But while they soaked up the details of the paintings, James remained fixated, staring at the statue.

He had barely moved since first clapping eyes on the magnificent lady, so Elouisa walked gingerly over to join him.

She was just about to ask what it was that had captivated him so when she too noticed something very, very familiar about the life-size carving. It was such a shock that it sent a shiver down her spine.

Held in the proud woman's hand was a clutch of what appeared to be straight sticks. Following her hand past the crook of her arm, around her neck was a beautiful necklace with a large central stone. On her pointing finger was a ring in the unmistakable shape of a corvid bird. Then draped over her arm wasn't a blanket as they had first thought, but a beautifully carved body length cloak, with a heavy hood and a very distinctive clasp.

M oses was hopping about, chattering in his native tongue, a strange blend of hyper excitement and pride at their find.

Henry couldn't really get what all the fuss was about. No fan of confined spaces, he had walked back out soon after exploring. He was now stretched out on a large rock, sun on his back, watching a family of giraffes in the far distance, his eyes being so much more attuned than the rest.

Behind him, hundreds of multi-coloured butterflies had started gathering around the entrance to the cave. The pattern on their wings was like a thousand eyes, a peacock glinting in the beams of the sun. They were clearly attracted to whatever was in the powder James had used. But it was as if they too had crowded in to pay homage to the home of the ancient African queen.

The girls were excitedly zooming about every nook and cranny, exploring the painting and looking for anything the others may have missed.

Their parents, however, were stumped by what they had found. Both privately thinking the same thing:

"How on earth could a statue carved by the world's most ancient race of shamanistic people, not only have such a detailed map of the world, thousands of years before its discovery, but how could it also contain images of the magical artefacts of their own family?"

Those precious items had been in their Cornish line, on the British Isles, thousands of miles away, for centuries? They had believed that they had actually been forged in ancient Britain.

James, in particular was stunned, for there was much about this statue of an incredibly proud and strong and clearly important woman that both enchanted and puzzled him.

He thought he had learned much about the San and Namib people and yet it was clear there was so much more to discover.

"She must have been a very powerful leader. A strong queen," said Moses, full of awe and pride himself.

"And that map, that map seems to prove that your people travelled the globe much earlier than the academics and teachers claim. Don't you see, Moses? They had boats. They didn't wait for the ice-bridges to cross to Europe and the other continents. They sailed," said Elouisa.

James smiled at his companion's infectious enthusiasm as he listened.

"Well, this is certainly a very important discovery, very important indeed. So pleased that we stumbled upon this together, my friend," he said, placing his arm around Moses' shoulders.

Elouisa was transfixed by the look on the woman's face, a confidence that implied that she could very well have been the

Earth Mother, creator of the universe. It was a look that once seen none would ever forget.

It was Holly's curious mind, however, that pointed out something they had all overlooked. She spotted it while examining the detail on what looked very like her own Rubyrobe.

Drawing everyone closer, she pointed to the statue's waist.

"Has anyone noticed this?" she said, indicating what looked like a short sword or perhaps a long dagger. "I recognise all the other items, of course. But what could this be? Alice and I have scanned every inch of this place and found nothing else here."

"It looks like some sort of knife," said Moses.

"But it is not the way my people would wear something like that, and it is no design I have ever seen. Come to think of it, neither does the ring or the cloak. And the creatures on the necklace make no sense. That is a dolphin," he said, pointing, "But this is far from the sea."

"Well, I have a hunch," responded James, "that each of these artefacts corresponds to a point on that world map.

"They may well be trophies that she and her tribe brought back from the corners of the globe.

"They may symbolise the fact that, once upon a time, Moses, your ancient people visited and then returned with great treasure from the very ends of the earth.

The old Druid was always stunned by these moments.

After such a long time away he was, once again, face to face with the seer.

The giant girl, Loriza lived here, in a cabin that, from the outside, resembled a tiny, dilapidated fisherman's shack. But approached from this entrance, it revealed its true nature, a room the size of a church, constructed from ancient henge stone.

She could not see the Druid, her keeper and mentor, but she, of course, knew that he was coming, as he always did. For she had special second sight and trust in his attentiveness.

So, she rose to her full height. She was an impressive sight, three times that of a normal man, let alone one so bent and broken by time and toil as he.

She held out her hands in a gesture of affection and Brinn walked forward and gently placed his wizened face between her palms.

"How are you, my precious girl?" he asked quietly, sensitive to the fact that she was no longer a youngster and disliked being treated like one.

"Oh, I am still weary, Oldfather," she whispered, in a voice that echoed in this cavernous space, "Always tired, for I am troubled by what I see, and I still see far, far too much."

With this she turned and wandered over to what appeared to be a large, stained glass window situated at her eye level.

Yet, when the observer looked closer, from this side, it was clear that this was no ordinary window. The characters and creatures and elements depicted were animated. They came alive and moved, enacting dramas and scenes in technicolour there on the wall.

"The ocular window, that portal on the world has been telling troubling things for many phases now, Oldfather. Something has upset the balance. A storm of crisis, a pandemic of plague and pain has come."

The old Druid shuffled forward, trying to decipher the patterns on the window. But as usual it made no sense to him, even though he had ancient wisdom and magical powers.

Only she, the blind, giant seer had the connection with the spirits to make sense of the dramas played out in the window. Her power came from her isolation. She had something to speak of whenever he called. But he had rarely seen her appear as disturbed as this.

"Behold," she announced, "the great poisoning of nature that mankind has wrought. The pandemic is here. The animals of the land, air and water, they suffer, they twist, they change. There is a seeping sickness that spills from the land into the sea. Weep for what you have done, I weep for what you have all done."

She now started to rock back and forth, her whimpering sounding to human ears like waves crashing on rocks. Tears streamed from the dark sockets that once were eyes. Air bubbled through her snaggled teeth, exiting at the dry corners of her chapped lips. She was clearly in deep distress.

The old man tried to console her as best he could. But he was visibly shaken by what she had just relayed.

The seer was a very particular type of special.

She had no love for people and never seemed to crave company.

But she had a unique gift of exceptional inner sight.

Ever since the crone took her eyes and independence, the power she was left with allowed her a glimpse into the dark places that opened rare doors to the future. And most worryingly for mankind, for as long as Brinn had been alive, which was a very, very long time, the seer had never ever, been wrong.

Brinn took a bundle of twigs from inside of his robe. It was sage, and he set it alight in the fire. He then walked about the cavernous space waving the smoke around. This was an ancient way of cleansing, of dispelling malevolent spirits and restoring some calm. He also had to believe that it might keep the crone from returning.

He then took his giant charge by her hand and steered her tenderly back to the wooden chairs.

She seemed relieved to be given a rest from the images in the window, which disturbed her so.

Brinn then set to the task of preparing a fresh meal, as he always did, this time a calming broth made from an infusion of herbs hanging over the ever-burning fireplace. A large bowl of soothing potion sometimes worked when she became agitated. It was a terrible burden of responsibility for the seer having to witness the things others don't see, even with a giant's heart and courage.

"Do you know?" she said softly, in between mouthfuls of the welcome meal. "I hear the seasons from here. The woodpeckers and plovers at day mark the end of winter and arrival of spring. Meadow larks nesting and song thrushes calling to mates herald the season of growth, while the bark of the Cornish chough and the murmurations of starlings tell me much about summer. By the seasons of mellow fruitfulness and passing, field pheasants, robins and owls bring me news throughout those long nights. But lately their voices have been fewer and the tales increasingly sad. For now, a rare ravenwind is blowing in from the west. And it bites bitterly."

Brinn touched the top of her great, hairy hands reassuringly as he replied, "Remember, my child, I live among those creatures and those winds, and while we have had some difficult seasons, the news is not all bad."

"Tell me about the whispering winds again, Oldfather."

He smiled indulgently. Then he took out a tin whistle and played for a few minutes, setting the tone. Finally, with a deep breath he sang soothingly, as he had countless times before.

"The larkwind is the wind at dawn, the owlwind at night.

The cuckoowind is the first wind of spring, swallowind brings summer in sight.

The rookwind heralds autumn, while starvelwind brings death.

The storkwind is the life-giver and the ravenwind the storm test."

She smiled then paused again, clearly thinking, then gulped back a deep breath and sighed her reply.

"I know you see the loss of the bees and the other flying insects too. I know you have smelt the stink of the poisons that cover the fields and lands, as I have, Earthfather. For few are so connected to the animals and the plants and the seas as the true Druids. But there is great trouble still from the Firehills that leech into the sea, Father. It must be stopped at source."

She paused, as if frightened to utter the next part.

"But we both know the cruelty of that source, the cruelty that prevented daughters from seeing and being with their father. We know that your guests have come and it will have alerted her. We also know that her wickedness this way comes and that she too will punish us for daring to love, to connect. We both know that even this dark fortress of ancient stones may no longer protect us."

Brinn could hardly lie to one with the power of inner sight. Even for reassurance. But that didn't mean he had to abandon his responsibility as a father to sugar the tough medicine in what he had to say next.

"It pains me every day, that you have to carry the heavy burden of second sight, daughter. But your visions are warnings, as you know, and your presence here keeps the peace.

While people have time, we all have opportunity to change things. We now have to find the source, convince people to change and to lead the way to correct the diseased magic. This is why I have lived so long, I can now see this, as you do."

The blind seer continued to face into her empty bowl while he spoke, perhaps nodding slightly at his reply or perhaps just moving her head.

He was right that she could not predict the future but was seeing what was most likely to occur. But knowing what she did of people and their ways, she did not hold out much hope for happy endings while the ancient hatred lived on in the sea wytch.

"Some news has come of support from an ancient place. Do

not lose hope, my child, do not despair."

He offered this news in an upbeat tone, hoping that it may kindle some form of belief.

But only silence echoed loud for several long seconds.

"Your broth was very good. Yet it has made me drowsy, Father. I must sleep, and you must leave before Mother returns from the other time. For if the sea wytch finds you with me, she will put me beyond reach forever, as she has long promised to do."

Brinn felt a tinge of sadness at hearing his daughter's reminder of his former partner's obsidian heart. It re-kindled the pain of their estrangement. It always pulled at his soul. But he knew that what she warned him off was right.

So, he took her by the hand again and led her to her modest resting place.

He stayed long enough to make her comfortable as she placed her head upon the huge pillow stuffed with the downy feathers from what must be a thousand ducks.

Then he re-stoked the fire, added more wood, gathered Skibbers again (who was chewing on the nethers of something unfortunate) and then made his way wearily to the door..

A last glance at the ocular window on the world revealed nothing. Without the seer's presence, it reverted to simple stained glass.

Just as he and the old cat made their way out, he stopped and took the great key from his pocket. With it, he also removed an object he had made especially for this trip, as he did every trip. It was a heart made from sticks selected from the ancient elder tree.

These totems were designed, not to keep people out of the room, but to stop what was on the other side with the seer from crossing into his domain.

He blessed it, kissed it then tied it carefully to the back of the door. And as the Druid locked the door, he muttered an ancient incantation.

Half the words he said were the spell of barring, but the other half was to summon the help and support of the bearer of the ancient artefacts, the faerie warrior, the keeper of the Ravenring. For it was likely that, sometime soon the power of that ring would be needed again.

M oses was convinced that Elouisa's dramatic decline was the result of the influence of the Tokoloshe.

He ranted at James about the demon sucking her soul. But try as he might he could not convince either James or his partner to listen.

"This is how it works. Now it is in her mind and is sucking on her soul, controlling what she thinks."

James was a patient man, but this was pushing his limits.

"Moses, I just don't see why it would have helped us as it did, protect us, only to destroy what it clearly idolises and worships. Its whole existence is dedicated to becoming the familiar of a magical mistress, a witch or a Wiccan like my wife. Makes no sense even if she is rejecting it."

The sudden decline in Elouisa's condition had happened when they stepped out of the cave. It was almost as if the conditions in there were keeping the poison in her system at bay, but she needed to stay within the range of the influence of the statue.

After talking with Moses, James walked back in. His wife was lying on one of the cot beds, resting. Then he noticed that, seated on a rock behind her was the Tokoloshe. Then he saw something dribbling from its mouth.

James tried to get close enough to examine it, but when he did, it disappeared. So, he focused on his wife.

She was seemingly much improved. With a bolt of shock, he noticed that, on one of her wrists, slumped by her side, she had a couple of puncture wounds. Something with sharp teeth had presumably been sucking at her blood.

James felt a flash of rage and called for his daughters. In a few short seconds, Alice had reversed the invisibility and Holly had managed to freeze the beastie to the spot.

"He looks terrified. Are you sure, Dad?"

James rubbed his jaw, not unlike Alice did when thinking.

"I need a closer look."

Taking the Tokoloshe outside, James could examine it much more closely. He was expecting dark red blood marks around its teeth and mouth. But he was puzzled when he noticed that the goo dribbling there was greeny-yellow.

Holly was the first to comment for what she saw brought back some unpleasant memories from the battle near Ashridge.

"How come the Tok has been drinking Firehills poison, Dad?" she asked, never one to miss a detail.

"Where has it come from?" said Alice, her forehead furrowed.

James looked his daughter in the eyes and smiled before answering.

"I don't know for sure, girls. But the only answer I can think of is that he has been draining it from your mother somehow. It must be what remained in her system, despite all of our efforts to purge the pollutants."

Alice now looked even more confused.

"What, the Tokoloshe has gone from being a demon, an enemy, to being...a friend?"

As she said this, she held out her hand as if to stroke it and narrowly avoided losing a finger.

"I would never go so far as to suggest that, Alice Boo." He laughed, as she snapped her hand away at pace. "But it certainly seems devoted to your mom. Perhaps the poison was blocking its attempted bond? But who knows, perhaps if we can find a way to channel the demon in the right way, even something as nasty as this may have something positive to contribute to our family's long story?"

Moses was watching all of this from the shadow of the cave and could not believe his ears or eyes. The Tokoloshe is, was and to his mind would always remain the immortal enemy of his people. It was not some sort of medicinal leech. As the healer of his tribe, he was sworn to detect and destroy every demon encountered before it created more of its kind.

As far as Moses was concerned, this creature had charmed this family somehow. It had probably enchanted them with its dark power. It was, and it remained an ongoing threat to these special people. But it also knew the secrets of the elephant graveyard, a place of great spiritual importance. And that meant it was a threat to the things he held dear.

"No", he thought. "There was only one thing for this. I must destroy the beast at the earliest opportunity. But I cannot do this on my own".

That night, the Savage family camped at the site of the African queen or goddess, while Elouisa continued to heal. Despite the children's discomfort at what the Tokoloshe appeared to be doing, the fact that no-one saw its macabre behaviour and the fact that their mother was clearly improving, meant they all turned a blind eye to the reality.

Moses volunteered to sleep in his tent above the car, and to guard the entrance, while the family enjoyed the shelter and healing powers of the sacred space.

They awoke with the dawn. The cave faced east, and the amethyst crystals turned the whole room an enchanted purple as the sun rose.

Only the Tokoloshe remained snoring when, wiping the sleep from her eyes and thinking of bacon sandwiches, Alice stepped outside.

She was looking forward to a morning chat with their guide and friend. But to her surprise, rather than discover Moses crouched over the camp stove, she found that both Moses and their safari van had vanished into the morning air.

Book 4:

Secrets of the Sea Wytch

L oriza's vision had shown her that a terrible catastrophe was still brooding in the Firehills and that somehow, the Savage children were the key to preventing it at source.

She also knew that the sea wytch, her own mother, was hell bent on destroying the family and with them, all hope of reversing the tragedy unfolding in the ocean.

L ucy had decided to spend the day at the beach with Nanna Jo and JJ. Today, Coverack was their destination.

One of their favourite spots on the Lizard coast, it has everything people dream of when they think of a Cornish fishing village.

Approached down a long and winding, agapanthus and fuchsia-lined steep road, a beautiful, azure sea stretches out before you, glistening rich with the promises of a scintillating English summer's day.

Yet when the tide is out, what seems like a mile of cream, powdery sand calls invitingly to families looking for fun in the Cornish sun.

Lucy chose a favoured spot between what they called seagull rock and the hand, a long, barnacle-encrusted lump of granite that looked like a fist standing proud of the now pooling water.

Lucy knew from experience that some of the best sea creature finds were to be made there, and she and her sisters always made for this spot when helping the coastal trust do their annual sealife census or count.

Despite being incredibly pretty, with the old lifeboat house and thatched fishing cottages marking the access point to the open ocean, there was so much to do, and windsurfers and kayakers were already setting out for a day of delights. There was a rumour that whale sharks and porpoises were in the area and people were understandably excited.

JJ now knew this place well, having grown up on these sands. He ran for the sea the second off his leash, scattering a raucous group of gulls on the way.

Lucy grabbed her belly board, having put on her black and pink wetsuit before they left Mermaid Cottage, and set off in pursuit of her furry friend.

NJ smiled indulgently, then set about the adult stuff, laying out towels and unpacking the yellow and grey pop-up tent that provided some much-needed shelter to keep lunch cool and ladies from sun burning.

As she did, she was pleased to see the smiling faces of their dearest friends Mark, Jane and Tait who had arranged to meet up with them today. They were staying in a beach house on the headland and bore a hamper of Elizabeth's legendary pasties as well as a fresh-baked, golden apple pie.

"Oooh!" said NJ excitedly, kissing Mark on his bald head. "Elizabeth's pastry really can't be beaten. The magic's all in the hands, you know. And I bet the apples came from the witch tree on the coastal path."

"No doubt," he laughed through his handlebar moustache, before taking over the shelter building. They had brought multi-coloured wind breaks too, but today was set to be a scorcher, by all accounts.

"You'll be thanking me for the shade when the sandcastle competition starts," Mark joked, patting his pocket where his design was tucked away.

Tait, meanwhile, had already joined Lucy and Jack in the water, throwing his t-shirt off on the way, much to his mum's irritation.

"Good job we pre-applied the sun-lotion," she laughed.

After a good half hour of watching Jack fetch his stick repeatedly, paddling like a miniature speedboat, the terrier eventually tired of the futility of the human's actions and stood over it, growling a warning not to chuck it again.

Just to be sure, much to their disgust, he quickly cocked his leg on it too.

So, they abandoned that game and took to the belly boards instead, wading out to where the breakers started, waiting for the best and then riding them back to the sand, shrieking with delight.

Tait was a bit faster than Lucy, as he had been on a surfing course the previous summer. But that was probably just as well, as on about the fifth go, Lucy caught a glimpse of something glinting beneath them in the water.

As she stared down, she jumped out of her skin when a face appeared. It was smiling.

Lucy instinctively fell from her board and behind her wave. As she was treading water, Jack doggy paddled up to her and started licking her face.

"Ugh!" she spluttered, but any other reaction was cut short as she was suddenly pulled under the salt water.

When she looked down in panic to see what had hold of her, she was relieved but a little irritated to see it was her sister, Savannah who was grinning as she whispered into her ear through the water. "Hello, Sis. I've got lots of news. But remember, Tait doesn't know everything about our special ways."

So, by the time Tait reached the shore, what he was greeted by was Lucy with her board under her arm and Savannah, in a peacock blue swimming costume, with the dog under hers and a warm smile on her radiant face.

He was puzzled by her sudden appearance. But their friend had long learned to ask no questions of the mysterious Savages.

Instead, he just smiled, shook his surfer's locks and suggested a race to Archie's Loft for a well-earned double choc-chip cone.

Wicca folk, also known as Wiccans or witches have had some very bad press down the centuries, and not just in the British Isles.

In the Americas, the so-called Puritans famously put many to death by crushing, burning and drowning them, the most infamous being the murders following the Salem witch trials.

Across Europe, countries employed witch finders to track magical folk down in towns and villages and they too met a typically grisly fate. And in Africa, witches are still persecuted to this day.

Anyone can be accused of witchcraft for simply being an outsider, a herb-healer or just different in some way. Having very white or albino skin or even a birthmark, can sometimes mean that people are singled out and subjected to great cruelty.

Cultures are afraid of magical people for a variety of reasons. People in power sometimes see the ancient healing and magical arts as a threat to the wealth and power of their own religion or beliefs. So, sometimes, they accuse Wicca or Pagan people of being in cohorts with evil, dark powers, demons and devils. This paranoia and malice is thought by many to be the origins of what is called black magic, malevolent magic intended to cause harm or distress.

Most children, however, understand that magic can be a wonderful thing when used for good. They know that ancient magic is at the heart of nature, which is far too incredible to have achieved all its bounteous beauty and majesty all on its own.

But if nature needs a seasoning of magic to reach its best; magic, when it goes wrong or is conjured with poor intent, can be a very destructive force too.

The changeling children had all experienced this when they had their family torn apart by the malicious crone. They had also witnessed its effects when parts of Ashridge Forest were polluted and poisoned, twisting and deforming the creatures that lived there.

Now it would appear that the same was happening to the sea here in Cornwall as the pandemic spread. And when problems happen at sea, thoughts turn automatically to the legend of the sea wytch.

Where shore Wicca turn to the forests, dales and possibly rivers and hills for the source of their power, sea witches or wytches look to the ocean, the flora and fauna of the water, beaches and the power of the moon as it commands the relentless tides.

Perhaps the most infamous sea wytch in this part of the coast had been their ancient grandmother. She once dominated the area. But she had not been seen on the peninsula since she cursed her own family and cast them adrift in the storm of alienation and despair that nearly destroyed them all, and from which they were still recovering.

Little had been heard of her, that was, until now. For on this very day, just a few bays round from glorious Coverack, a hunched figure with a face lined by self-loathing and spite, crabbed through the long tunnel of windswept trees along the coastal path that meandered past the secret passageway to her lair.

She was oblivious to the beauty of the tunnel created by the gorse on the path or the beauty of the view. For her heart was black, you see, and selfish and cruel, so much so that children and small animals fled at the sight of her.

Her selfish ears were blocked to the sweet sound of baby laughter or children at play. Her nose was long dead to the wonderful scent of crushed apples under the ancient Pippin tree or the wild herbs and garlic that lined the path.

Her leathery skin long shunned the tender touch of the seaside sun and she travelled slowly but relentlessly, like a virus spreads, unseen.

Flowers fade in her wake, shutting their petals protectively like they do when dusk casts its long shadow or when winter frost comes too soon.

Even the rare diamond-backed adders slithered for cover as she approached, and father rabbits lay low in their burrows or the undergrowth, paws over the anxious mouths of their young in case she heard their frightened gasps. For this crone spoke with the sound of fairies crying, spat spite for words and was known to use fresh bones in her conjuring, counting no-one among her friends.

Her destination was a place aptly situated on a crossroads. Three paths led to the pleasure of beach, ancient temple-rocked headland or wild abandoned surf. The fourth road, however, led west and skirted with misery, mockery and pain. For this road was her wretched domain.

And sure enough, she bled slowly down that path less trodden. The sea wytch's destination was the distant cabin, hiding in plain sight, known locally as the fisherman's hut near Black Head.

Yet here, unbeknown to anyone, (because, for reasons nobody could ever recall, nobody had ever entered the hut), the lonely giant Loriza rested her too-busy mind.

Inside the dark confines of her cell, the gentle giant girl lay on her cot, weeping. For she knew what was coming.

She deeply feared her ancient mother and the cold, cruel wickedness that was stretching its dead fingers towards her throat.

She knew what the omens had conjured as her fate and despite all of her power, she was terrified at what was in store for them all in the grasp of those bony, alienating hands.

Mohbreen's malevolence was the stuff of the darkest nightmares of Cornish fisher folk and villagers alike. Although few knew her true name and even fewer spoke of her, for fear of her spite and wrath.

She was believed to have had a hand in most shipwrecks or tempests, famines or floods on this coast. For it is said that the ancient race of sea wytches can control the very elements and thus can sometimes command the wild ocean itself, bringing wrecker's bounty when treasure or food was scarce.

Despite her notoriety, she could still shuffle through the shadows of the villages and towns, forests and meadows with few paying her much heed, hiding her spite in plain sight with wicked craft.

Yet she always watched and was wary of the children.

The few who know the history of the ancient Trelgathwin family, would recall the origins of her malice as depicted in the

Legend of the Lost. But outside the Savages now, and the sea gypsies or perhaps the witchcraft museums, her dark ways were mostly hidden in the dusty corners of the annals of time.

Nobody knew that she had been holding her own daughter, the seer, captive for a very long time in the hope that, one day, the giant girl gifted with second sight would lead her back to her true quarry, her stolen second and favourite daughter, Elouisa.

But until she had the chosen one back where she belonged, her bubbling wrath would make all who crossed her suffer. And this suffering, she knew, would bring her true heir closer to her return. For it was her daughter's fate to inherit the dark magical path and power she had chosen for her, on the black night she and her monstrous twin were born and promised to the darkness.

Double-blessed with the power of the ancient ones, Elouisa was truly Wiccan-bonded. Her father too came from a long magical line. He was of ancient Druidic stock. This meant that Elouisa possessed a very special blend of powers.

Her sister, on the other hand, initially showed no signs of being blessed in that way. Instead, she soon grew deformed, withered and diseased.

Sadly, their father was forced to leave when the pull of the darkness became too strong for his wife to resist and she began to shut him out. He also feared her intentions towards the less favoured daughter.

So he took their other daughter, the damaged one. But after he left, after this betrayal, his wife became increasingly bitter and twisted. She fast grew racked with a misery, self-loathing and pain that she could have overcome with kindness and strength of character. But instead, she turned from the light of the fae and chose the dark, alienating path of the vindictive and the cruel. The Book of the Dead became her only reference guide.

Today, cloaked in that wickedness, her presence was spreading slowly but ominously to the lowly fishing shack on the cliff side.

The sea wytch now crept up to the hut's slightly pathetic wooden door, bleached pale by the sun and sea spray. She slowly mounted the few creaking steps to the porch deck, then reached above the frame for the hidden key.

Meanwhile, inside, Loriza had awoken and sat upright on her modest bunk. She knew what was in store for her and she was waiting for the inevitable abuse to start again.

Loriza had been a slave to the will of the sea wytch for as long as she could remember and had come to dread their rare encounters. For the old woman, in her dry voice, always asked the same questions that she simply couldn't answer.

When the wooden door finally creaked open, bringing a sharp tang of sand and sea, the seer, Loriza sensed once again what was on the tip of the witch's tongue before she recited the nagging incantation of inquisition. It was as if she ignored the madness that the outcome of this visit would somehow be any different from the hundred before.

"So, tell me, damaged daughter of mine, who looks where darkness dares not spread. Where is your wretched sister? Where does she now lay her wicked head?"

The sea wytch said nothing else. She choked her voice and simply watched her blind face intently for what seemed like an age.

It soon became obvious, however, that there was to be no satisfactory answer forthcoming from that dark mouth and those empty eyes.

So, she sighed, shook her head wearily, took a glass phial from her cloak and limped over to the bed where her daughter slumped. Then, as the frightened woman lamented her torment at the controlling sea wytch's cruel hands, Mohbreen struck her sharply across the face. She then reached down deftly and, sniggering with a catch in her dry breath, captured her poor daughter's first falling tear.

She held it up to the light from the ocular window.

The phial was now half full.

She smiled through yellow teeth,

"Finally, I have enough," she spat, then shuffled toward the other door, cackling like dry logs on a hot fire.

"If you will not answer me, then I shall make the old man spill the secrets of the seer. I can smell his presence here. But first, time to finally remove the wretched seal that has restrained me from coming home all these years."

Tipping the phial of tears until it wetted the tip of her forefinger, she carefully traced the outline of the door with the precious unction. As she did this, she muttered something gutteral beneath her breath and the door started to buckle and creak as if resisting a strong flame. The strong wood and charms inevitably gave way to the power of her dark and tragic magic with a crack. Then the heavy lock was sprung, and the exit unbarred.

"NO!" came a booming cry from across the cavernous room.

The giant girl stumbled across the floor, sending her table flying. But she fell and could tell by the empty sound and musty smell that she was now too late.

By the time she made it across to the door, the sea wytch was through that broken portal and gone. The defeated warding charms now sadly lay scattered about the floor, the heart broken underfoot like pathetic match sticks.

Having been confined to one room for most of her life, Loriza, despite her giant size, simply couldn't summon up the courage to cross the threshold. It stung her like a thousand nettles to even try.

So, she resolved to do the one thing she did better than anyone else. She turned to face the ocular window, to see what fate had in store following this unexpected turn of events. For this was a dark plan that the wytch had somehow hitherto managed to hide from her daughter's second sight.

At first the visions were chaotic, like they were still adjusting to a shift in the grand scheme of nature. But then, they began to take on a new, a fresh order.

First, she saw the dark figure shuffling up the long secret passageway to the house where Brinn lay sleeping, seemingly unaware of the fate that was in store for him. But this scene cut away before it concluded, before her unwitting father's fate was revealed.

Then the picture changed to a barren and warm land where the changeling family fought a battle for their very lives.

They appeared to be trapped in a walled tomb and as the

serried ranks of the dark shaped forces closed in on them, the walls of their fortress seemed to become their prison. The cave appeared to crumble and collapse, making her pulse race and heart strain at her chest with anxiety.

But despite her trepidation, she forced herself to watch on.

The vision shifted to the emerald seas, the other side of this door. It was a sunny summer's day. Tranquil turquoise waters. Yet swarms of black birds descended and pecked mercilessly at what appeared to be the corpses of pile upon pile of sea creatures, drying horribly in the sun.

She knew that these distressing scenes were all acts in a great play and were all connected in some way. That they were lines written but not yet enacted.

She also suspected that the common link, the dark source of poison, had just left this room.

What she had seen this time seemed to be less of a vision and more a threat. It wasn't so much a prediction and more of a portent, a warning. For only the seer was gifted with the power to glimpse into the future and possibly alter it if she dare. But only if she was wise and brave enough to know just what to change and was willing to pay the demanded and inevitable price for playing with providence.

Hers was a gift that sat heavily upon the shoulders of someone so large in stature but so modest in means and courage. She may have looked gigantic to some, but there was still a little girl trapped within that huge frame.

Sickened by what she saw, she summoned up her every reserve of strength by picturing again and again the plight of the special people in peril in her vision. These were her kin, her kind. The vulnerable were her lost family. Their unmet spirits gave her hope and courage, but for how long?

Then, as if fearing faith would falter, with a cry of pain that took the last of her resolve, she managed her first excruciating step through the portal door into the cruel outside world.

This was the first time that she had been outside of her room in almost a lifetime. And how sad that this act, for such a gentle giant, was not about to be met with love, but was akin to inserting her foot into a cauldron of boiling water.

Henry scanned the horizon from the top of the highest ridge he could find in the Twyfelfontein valley.

But he could still see no sign of Moses.

It took it out of him, more than usual, to adopt his changeling form during the day. But the urge to run free in the African savannah was too much to resist. He had particularly enjoyed racing the female cheetah as she pursued an impala on his way to this vantage point. He had, of course, lost to Africa's fastest cat. But it had been a close-run thing.

As he scanned the horizon, he thought he saw what looked like a cloud. He dismissed it at first for a dust devil, a natural mini whirlwind. But then it moved steadily and slower than he would have expected the wind to move. So, he set off to investigate, alternating between running on two long legs and four, a sort of loping run.

The going was relatively easy now as the pads on his feet spread to give him added purchase in the sand. Occasionally he would have to leap over rocks and screed and the odd tuft of dried, brown grass, but it was mostly open territory. He had seldom felt so alive and so free, especially when a herd of curious wildebeest mistook him for a predator and scattered in all directions, several out-pacing him for a good mile or so.

With his mind returning to the task at hand, he surfed down one dune then scaled another and trained his eyes, ears and sensitive nose on the same spot up ahead.

He was panting heavily now, not because he was out of breath, but as a way to cool down. For werebeasts, like dogs, can't sweat to manage their body temperature.

"Yes, there it is again", he thought, but this time he could see that the smoke was in fact dust and that it trailed behind three vehicles.

He recognised one instantly. It was their off-white safari truck. But he was then in for a shock, as alongside their truck was the same battered bakkie they had sent packing a day or two before. This time, however, it was completely packed out with bodies, front and back. It was also accompanied by another, carrying at least six others and they appeared to have guns, many guns.

Henry watched them for a few minutes to make sure of his fears. But "no, there could be little doubt", he thought, "they are heading straight for my family, as if someone is guiding them". And sadly, to his mind, there could only really be one person who that someone could be.

The look on his father's face spoke volumes as Henry returned, shaking with fury at the bad news he had to relay.

"Yes, Moses is leading the poachers here?" he repeated, his voice betraying hurt as much as anger, not being someone renowned as a poor judge of character.

"Sounds like they're heavily armed as well, which leaves us little choice." James added.

"What?" said Elouisa, suddenly animated, mind whirring. "You're not seriously suggesting we run, and leave all of THIS, are you?"

She was looking him straight in his eyes, searching for any sign of weak resolve.

"Well, I'm not planning to make a stand with our children, against a dozen or more crazed poachers armed with assault rifles and, for all we know, fully briefed on us and our "special" gifts. Especially as you're still drained. Are you thinking clearly?"

Elouisa marched over to the goddess statue before speaking again.

"You know what they will do with her and with the semi-precious stones covering these walls. I'm pretty sure that's gold in her necklace, there may be actual opals and diamonds too."

She was running her hands lovingly over the statue as she spoke.

"You're the archaeologist. We have a duty to this precious heritage, let alone the connection to our family, which we still need to fathom."

James, characteristically, remained calm and unflappable, although clearly conflicted.

"We can't put the children at risk. There can be no showdown as there was…."

"At the forest?" Elouisa shouted, finishing the sentence he was reluctant to.

"Well…yes!"

"James, you are a warlock from a direct line of magic users that pre-dates the arrival of the Romans in Britain. There is nothing that can truly compete with that."

He was quiet for a few minutes then raised his head and answered.

"But you did. You almost killed me. And were it not for massive support, all would have been lost."

He had half expected her to baulk at this reminder, but she smiled lovingly instead.

"Well, perhaps we can summon help again?"

He held her gaze and was, as ever, impressed by the determination she could summon at will.

"The sensible answer has to be to re-seal the entrance and

make our way back to the base camp."

"But who is to say they won't blast it open? Moses knows exactly where the entrance is. Even if we enchant it, he has special sight and powers of his own. Remember he is from sangoma stock? He is a shaman too."

She decided to press her case further.

"Even if we do make it back and in good time and this place holds, if they are frustrated here what do you think they will do next?

"Moses knows the way to the sacred grounds of the elephants, the reason why the poachers were here in the first place? Dinganwe and the guardians will be no match for those automatic rifles. All of them have huge motivation, especially after what we've done to frustrate them."

James had to admit to himself, she made a compelling case.

Holly had been listening in silence, along with her siblings. She took her father's hand and then her mother's.

"I have an idea," she said. "Please, just trust me."

Fusion elemental can only happen when the magic users all have the same motives or goal. It is a way of combining or blending powers so that the magic force produced is greater than the sum of the individual parts. It proves the power of working together. And Holly had learned about it from watching a favourite children's film.

"Look, it's worth a go," she said, to doubting looks from Alice in particular, who always took some convincing when it came to something new.

"The idea is we blend our powers and you and Pops use the extra energy to summon the same elemental forces that formed the sand dunes and craters, to carve a maze of different caverns that Moses simply won't be able to follow."

She had that characteristic look of determination signalling that "no" wasn't an option.

"Of course, the crystals will amplify our power. And when has anyone seen more crystals than here? Even Savannah's cave can't match this place."

After a brief conference between the parents, not able to think of anything better, the family formed a semicircle around the statue of the earth goddess and joined hands while Henry watched the progress of the poacher convoy from above.

Elouisa led the incantation, focusing on the beautiful face of the goddess as she channelled nature's power. Eventually, as she muttered rhythmically, Alice joined her and a bright ray of light formed at the joining of each pair of hands. It then sprayed out toward the amethyst walls.

Here the light refracted in peaks and prisms and turned from gold to purple, shattering into a thousand shards of energy. James then instinctively harvested these fragments and somehow directed the stream of energy out beyond the cave door.

By visualising what he wanted to create, he set the shards of light about the work of his imagination. They were bustling like magical worker bees in the air and termites along the ground.

Remarkably swiftly, walls of mud and rock were being constructed, creating an earthen maze where once there had simply been sand and air.

The single, hard-baked former riverbed path became manifold, each new path leading in random directions but directing the unwitting traveller right back to the start.

While these magically elemental workers set about creating this alternative landscape within their landscape, the earthen maze, the four magic-using members of the family maintained their close connection, the force passing through each of them like an electric current of Wiccan power.

When Henry looked down he was, at first shocked to see his

parents and siblings lit up in this way, golden and purple light obscuring their eyes and mouths. But he could see that they were smiling with joyous concentration, admiring the sensation of the magic flowing through them and their joint handiwork like painters or abstract artists or engineers.

In all of an hour, the raised mud maze was complete and wet earth was baking in what was left of the hot afternoon desert sun.

From his vantage point, Henry could see the multiple entry points to the earthen maze and how impossible it would be for anyone to successfully navigate their way in or through it.

By the time he came down to rejoin his family, the adults were resting, clearly drained by their efforts, while the girls giggled together, exhilarated by their exertions.

What none of them had noticed, however, was the change that had taken place to the goddess statue.

During the convergence, the stone had changed colour in places and her hair was now glowing like serpentine, jet black with sparkling crystals.

Most notably, two of the icons on the map were now glowing, the Willowand and Rubyrobe.

It was clear that a metamorphosis, a dramatic transformation was happening. But none of them quite understood what that would mean for this place, for the family, or the world stretching out beyond them.

Moses was driving the safari van, trying to recall the route back to the cave. This was made a great deal more difficult because there was a rusty gun barrel in his ribs likely to go off any second.

He had been driving to the home of a tribe he knew well, when he was ambushed.

Deeply troubled by the Tokoloshe, he needed the advice of the powerful mentor sangoma, the leader of the tribe whom he knew well and who had a reputation as a demon hunter. But he never made it there.

The poachers had already visited the village and had been waiting for an elephant caravan, until he happened to stumble upon them instead.

Recognising the van, they quickly overpowered Moses and demanded he take them to the elephant's sacred place of legend. But rather than lead them there, which he knew would lead to carnage, he chose to take them to his European friends who, having outsmarted them once, could no doubt do it again.

He had not, however, expected there to be so many, their

numbers having grown since their last encounter. And he was now very, very scared.

Everywhere he looked, faces of evil stared back. Pockmarks, missing teeth and deep scars typified the poacher, no doubt mauled by creatures fighting back or from fighting each other.

They were a filthy bunch and yet worse still were hell-bent on revenge for how the Savage family had frustrated them to date. So, this time they had come armed, with a shaman of their own, the same sangoma Moses had gone to find and who was also a captive of the poachers now.

He was riding in one of the battered bakkies, in full witch doctor regalia; leopard skin head dress, lion claw necklace and assegai or spear with zebra tail tassel. His face was painted with chalk-white mud, giving him the appearance of a waking ghost.

Moses slowed the vehicle as they approached where he remembered the entrance to the riverbed canyon should be. But instead, they were now faced with half a dozen optional paths.

Rather than betray any sort of hesitation and face the guns again, Moses chose to place his trust in his mystical friends and elected to take the first path on the left. But before he drove on, he wound down his window and told the driver of the other cars that they should take a path each, so they would have a better chance of encountering their quarry if they tried to flee.

He was acting on a hunch but felt instinctively that he should divide the poacher force.

Moses then slowed the car to virtually walking pace as they pressed on. In his car, he had the poacher leader and five of his people, including a very nasty woman with crocodile claws in her hair. He had managed to divide their force, but they were still more than he could handle on his own.

Having seen his friends in action before, however, he sensed that they would now not be very far away.

The first of the poachers to realise that something was wrong were the vermin riding in the back. One minute they were there. The next time he looked in his rear-view mirror they had gone. And they were taken without so much as a scream.

The men in the front seat, however, were so tense at driving through the claustrophobic, looming canyon that they didn't even notice. They sensed nothing even when Alice let a few flying sparkles slip accidentally as she flew in silently through the open window, shrunk them with the Willowand and then carried them off in her pockets.

On a hunch, after a few hundred yards, Moses claimed that there was something wrong with a tyre and stopped the car. This gave him the opportunity to get the remaining poachers, and their leader, out of the vehicle.

As Moses and the leader walked round to the suspect wheel, Henry entered the car in the blink of an eye from the other side where he dragged the two remaining poachers away over the dune, this time very much screaming with fear.

This left a bemused looking leader alone with his captive, Moses, who fancied these odds considerably more, especially as the poacher was now holding a wriggling cobra where once he held a gun.

"Ayeeeee!" screamed the gold-toothed villain, dropping the serpent on the floor and starting to run.

"Not so fast," said Moses, clearly furious at what had almost befallen them all at the hands of these human monsters.

As the man ran, sprinting for his life, Moses reached into the roof of the van and with the same motion drew his knobkerrie and hurled it after the poacher. He caught him smartly behind his right ear, knocking him out cold.

Soon, with the leader of the poachers securely bound and the rest rounded up by his magical friends, they were back together and navigating the true path back to the cave, which now magically appeared before them.

"Clever, so, so clever," Moses laughed, energised by the battle, his beaming laugh, teeth and twinkling eyes flashing with relief and pride.

"I knew that you would find a way, I knew. Why did I ever doubt you?"

On route, they passed one of the rusty bakkies and what appeared to be Elouisa's Everbag. From the shouts and screams echoing from inside, it was clear that it was now a makeshift magical cell for the former inhabitants of that car.

As they rounded the final bend in the mystical mud maze, however, they were shocked to see a strange figure standing before the cave.

James's heart started to race when confronted with another, seemingly malevolent sangoma, now guarding the entrance to the goddess cave. And what was worse, standing in front of him, a huge grin on its face, was the creature Moses loathed more than hell itself. Yes, once again it was the dreaded Tokoloshe demon.

Brinn had anticipated this day for decades. He just wasn't feeling up to confronting it today.

But there was no doubting the disturbance in the sonar clicking of the bat guards signalling the passing of a malignant presence that could only mean one thing. The day of reckoning was upon him.

He reached into the chimney breast and removed his golden-handled sickle and straw pentangle which he fastened to the concealed door.

He then pulled back the seagrass rug on the floor to reveal the compartment containing his hidden henge and quickly assembled the crystals and stones, each corresponding with the 12 touchstone points. There was a different crystal for every month: garnet, aquamarine, amethyst, diamond, emerald, pearl, ruby each in their power positions, each balancing its opposite in order to channel their goodness in equilibrium.

He didn't have to look out of the window to know that the sun had passed over the harbour hill, which would mean he would be denied its additional power charge. Of course, she would have known this and timed her arrival when his strength was beyond its zenith, but hers charged by the pending night.

Reaching for a large glass bowl, he filled it with water from the blessed well. Then he carefully balanced a sizeable chunk of crude magnesium ore on the shelf above it.

Finally, the ancient Druid took up his oaken staff that held the smooth granite ball and, whispering an incantation into the claw that was rather like blowing out a candle, he set it spinning. This conjured a light that his plant guards responded to, barring all possible exits with bark and branches.

For some reason, the last thing he was expecting was for his former love to actually knock before entering. At this unexpected but chilling announcement, before he had time to react the door started wobbling and distorting until finally it buckled to one side.

He wasn't entirely surprised when the pathetic pentangle charm simply withered to nothing on the floor. For hers was the most malign of all powers. It was fuelled by the great shade writ large in The Book of the Dead. He was facing a true adversary now.

"You disappoint me, old man," she taunted. "Trinkets and tokens? Do you forget that my lineage has Druidic roots as well?"

He was seated in his great wooden chair by the ever-roaring fire and simply continued to stare stoically into the face of the onslaught he had expected. In these moments, appearance of calm was more important than control itself.

As she made to enter the room, she encountered an invisible

energy shield that came from the combined force of the protective enchantments. But reaching into her robes, she produced the potent phial of tears for the second time that day, and with a flick of the long nail of her index finger sprayed the contents onto the crystals, extinguishing their flow like snuffing a candle.

She then unceremoniously stepped over the circle with greater agility than any onlooker would have expected.

"The Mighty Brinn Elder reduced to these illusions. You really are a pitiful loser," she hissed.

But as she did, he flicked the oaken staff with a snap of his wrist and the block of magnesium fell into the water producing a sudden but intensely blinding flash in the gloom.

This threw the wytch backward, enabling him to rise like the fox he once was and draw the sickle about her throat.

"Now, I think that is quite enough, oncewife," he whispered, in a low but assertive voice.

"Are you going to tell me why you have come and what it is going to take to make you return from whence you came?

"Or must I end you?

"For, as guardian of the gateway, you know that, despite our past association and yes, mostly because of it, I shall not let your disease pass through this way while breath yet fills my lungs."

The fact that he was talking and not acting was an encouraging sign for the canny dark magic user. She now played her best and most potent card with the illusion of a kind heart, that of the hapless and reformed victim.

"Now, my love. I know that you know that you won't harm

me. Lest we both forget, we created so much together."

She tried to turn to look him in the eyes, but he wouldn't let her.

"And she is why I am here, Daddy. I simply want to know where my precious daughter has gone."

As anticipated, this faux affection caused him to relax and soften his guard just slightly, just enough for her to gain the merest advantage. Before he could react, as quick as a viper strike, she sunk her black, poisoned Wiccan dagger into his old thigh.

Brinn dropped his sickle and cried out in pain.

Indeed, were it not for the timely intervention of his ginger tom leaping, spitting and clawing at her face from the top of the bookshelf, she probably would have finished the deadly deed there and then, sending him into the waiting arms of his ancestors.

In his distress and agony, he just about managed to cast the desperate shielding spell around himself that also barred her access to the gateway or portal door, her ultimate goal.

But his physical strength, his stamina would fade fast, and she knew it.

With a wave of her hand, the spent cat crumpled to the floor. Then, watching her former love gulping like a frightened fish in a bowl as he bled out, she stepped over the carnage and, quite unexpectedly set the kettle on the range to boil.

"Well, husband. If I am going to watch you fade away before I start my hunt, we may as well be civilized about the last of our down time together.

"Now, remind me, where do we keep the brew leaves in our kitchen? It's been a while."

L oriza's vision had shown her that a terrible airborne disease, a polluting pandemic was still brooding in the Firehills, that it was poisoning the earth and that somehow, the Savage children were the key to preventing it at source.

She also knew that the sea wytch, her own mother, their grandmother, was hell bent on destroying the family and with them, all hope of reversing the tragedy unfolding in the forest and the ocean.

For decades, the worst of the sea wytch's dark power had been frustrated and contained by the guardians. She had largely been trapped the other side of the portal, walking a nether world, caught in time, between the veils, undetected by many. But her influence had started to leech through the veil and was spreading.

If she broke through fully, if she accessed the portal, the gateway to the current world, cutting through space and time, not only would the poison suffocate the globe, but her sister Elouisa and everyone she loved would be doomed. And worse still, the elder wytch would force all to the Shadow Lands for good.

For although the ancient Wiccan race seldom embraces darkness and destruction, there is a fine divide between their light and the power of the shade. And this final portal lay at her father's door.

So, despite the agonising pain in every step, the brave, sightless giant was now slowly feeling her way along the slimy, damp walls.

Cobwebs clung to her face, spiders climbed into her hair and bats clicked what she took for a form of encouragement. But still she forced herself onward and upward to a destination she imagined but couldn't see.

D own in south west Africa, things had taken a very odd turn. Having been deployed as Elouisa's familiar or magical companion, a role it was all too keen to fulfil, the odiously hungry Tokoloshe had dispatched the rest of the poachers with aplomb.

He had had a little help from the others, of course, guns being turned to sticks, spears to flowers and car wheels suddenly running into quicksand, courtesy of the magical clan. But most of the actual nasty business had been this little beast's affair. And now, deep in her Everbag, Elouisa had safely stashed what was left of the bloodied, gagged, bound and frightened bandits.

The sangoma, in his tribal finery, was the last of the raiding party to be rounded up by the demon, who had chased him to the cave.

Still, he had taken some gathering and was now staring, wide-eyed, stunned at what he must have considered the many pale demons surrounding him.

Judging by his chanting and chattering, he wasn't about to give up easily, either.

As the Tokoloshe growled and grinned, the witch doctor spat a cloud of white powder in its face. But all it did was make the mini monster sneeze.

Then when he raised his assegai spear, it backed off, almost bored, with a frumpy growl.

"Get behind me, DEMON!" the shaman shouted, his bead and bone bracelets rattling as he tried to circle to a place where his back was covered. As he did so, he almost stumbled over the Willowand in Helygen guise. This time, the magical creature had transformed itself into a small brown snake licking its lips with a forked tongue. It was also burping purple stars.

"Aeeee!" the sangoma screamed, leaping in the air rather than tread on this reptile. "Another demon."

He swiftly reached into the pouch about his waist with his long fingers and scattered what looked like a collection of mummified animal parts, stones and twigs in a semicircle, seemingly creating a magical barrier between himself and his tormentors.

Just then, Henry returned, deftly moving from four legs to two and then from wolf into boy, in as little time as it took to mouth those words. This caused the sangoma to whimper audibly with terror.

Then, as Henry stopped at his sister's side, he smiled mischievously at the witch doctor, flashing his still sparkling teeth.

"They take some getting used to, but they are lovely people really," said Moses, approaching the skittish shaman from the man's blind side. "Please trust me. They are here to do good and now you are with us, we have something very special to share with you, old friend."

Seldom has anyone looked so relieved to see a familiar face. But as Moses stepped over the enchanted bone barrier, the sangoma still appeared concerned. This time it was that Moses had just deliberately broken his spell with ease and his confidence plummeted further.

He was peering nervously at the Tokoloshe, who had not taken its eyes off him since he had arrived.

"But what about…...?"

He nodded at the pig-like gremlin.

"Sheeesh! Him?" said Moses, exhaling his hidden disapproval.

"I cannot get used to it, I will not tell a lie. But so far, the beast has been more help than problem. And yes, look," he said, pointing to his sandled feet, "I still have all of my toes, despite sleeping near to it for more nights than I care to recall."

They all laughed, bar their guest.

At this, the Tokoloshe too appeared to grin, before following Elouisa back into the special cave they had just worked so hard to protect.

James and Moses embraced warmly, and swift introductions were made to each of the children in turn. The sangoma, Houngane, greeted the family gingerly. He was very reluctant to shake Henry's hand, in particular and shied away from the creature now on Alice's shoulder, which appeared to have sprouted legs.

Still feeling apprehensive, he did allow Moses to usher him toward the cave, explaining how it had been discovered. But as soon as they were inside, and his eyes had adjusted to the gloom from the brightest of sunlight, all his fears melted away. The soothing sight of the great earth goddess instantly dropped him to his knees.

"This is…. this is incredible. Do you realise who this is?" He cast this question to everyone in the room, joy on his face.

"She is Teote, ancient mother of the sun and of the moon. She is omnipotent. The shape changer. The Creator. She is holy of holies to all of my people."

He was smiling widely now. "Look," he cried, removing his animal hide tunic to reveal an intricate tattoo of a chameleon on his back, etched out in short, dark lines. "This is her symbol, for it is widely known that she changes form and colour, mood and shape to bring the seasons and reflect all terrains and peoples."

Suddenly the obscure creature on the drawing of Africa made more sense now. It was more than just a series of circles; it was a reptile and not just any reptile. It was the shapeshifting chameleon.

"And behold," cried the shaman. "She has come among us."

He was pointing toward the statue.

There, sure enough, on one of her out-stretched arms, now sat a beautiful, slate-green chameleon.

It was slowly soaking everything in with its huge eyes and inquisitive reptilian brain.

Then suddenly the chameleon, Helygen, nonplussed, darted his long tongue out and he caught an unfortunate moth dancing too near one of the torches as if it was the most natural act in the world.

Lucy was playing boules on Coverack beach with the ladies and their friends, when the messenger arrived. Ironically, JJ had just pinched the white Jack ball when Lucy felt the Ravenring tighten and then a butterfly landed on her shoulder...

Savannah noticed and heard the same message in her inner ear. Soon the sister's eyes met, just as Tait pulled the soggy sphere from the terrier's mouth.

NJ noticed the message pass between the siblings, and wasn't surprised when her granddaughter whispered in her own ear when nobody was listening, "We are going to have to go, we think Brinn is in a lot of trouble and we have to answer the call."

So, with fear in her heart, she reluctantly made an excuse about the girls having to fetch some more friends and hesitantly waved them off mouthing "be careful".

This was much to Tait's disappointment. But this was tempered, of course, by getting to be the terrier's guardian for the remains of the day.

The girls jogged to the pretty harbour wall then, once out of sight, Lucy borrowed a kayak from the surf school while Savannah swiftly changed form.

Soon they were cutting through the surf to Mousehole, stunning the odd windsurfer and lone fisherman en route as the kayak was propelled at quite a rate of knots.

Leaving their boat in the care of their dolphin friends, it was a fairly short run up the long lane to the cottage, the same spot they had occupied a day ago.

At this point, the girls realised that they had absolutely no idea what was going on and not the faintest idea of a plan.

As they looked at each other and were deciding what to do next, they were overjoyed to see four familiar faces appear over the hedge. Nelson, Ziggy, One-eyed Stanley and Madame Rebecca, were all armed to the teeth. They too had clearly received the winged message.

The pirate leader was humming a variation of the song Two Little Boys:

"Didya think we would leave you cryin', when there's room in our gang for two?"

"Well, well, well, luvverlies. Seems an old friend has an ancient problem, eh girls? Shall we? After you," and with his usual, suave theatrical style, he bowed and gestured towards the door with a long sweep of a sleeved arm.

"Are we glad to see you?" gasped Lucy, throwing her arms around Nelson while he smiled sweetly at Savannah who, as usual, was being slightly coy.

"Now les nat go rousin' the ole 'ouse as you two did last time you were ere, eh?" muttered Rebecca, a blunderbuss in her hands and a cutlass tucked into a crimson sash.

"Praps we is best findin' another way in?"

Just then, as if summoned by the tension, the same field mouse who met the girls before appeared at the foot of the hedge.

"You need to take great care," he said, in a tiny voice.

"All sorts of mystical going on has been happening in there all day. It's blocked off our front way in. You'll have to go around the back. But be warned, that wretched and cruel crone has fetched up in the cottage and she's trouble, mark my words she is. I've heard her crunch the bones of kin in her teeth."

Reluctantly, their tiny companion led the party quietly round the back where the old, lean-to greenhouse stood, missing panes and looking deliberately dishevelled, even haunted.

"It looks like it's falling down, but it's alright inside," said the mouse. "You can get in through here and then there's just the back door which he never locks because nobody ever comes."

Lucy crouched down and whispered, "That's twice you've helped us now, little friend. We'll remember your courage."

Pirates to the fore, with cat-like tread the small party filed delicately into the rear of the dilapidated cottage.

As Ziggy stole forward to try the handle on the back door, Savannah was hatching her own plan. She had noticed a water butt by a down drainpipe, and with some deft movements of her hands was fashioning something from the captured water. This caught the attention of the rest of the gang, pausing before committing to opening the door.

In no time at all, Savannah brought the liquid to life. Before them now stood a water golem. Operating it like a marionette, she marched it toward the threshold.

"Open it now," Rebecca called to Ziggy, who did as he was told while standing to one side.

They were wise to send the animated warrior in first, for the sea wytch had clearly sensed the magic in the wind and traps were waiting.

They felt the breeze from a blast a split second before seeing it and then all hell broke loose. It seemed like everything that wasn't nailed down suddenly flew and crashed into the body at the door.

While their watery warrior fortunately absorbed that blast, the pirates took the initiative and smashed through the kitchen windows. Savannah manoeuvred her charge a few steps further in but could feel him slipping in the face of stronger magic and she knew that her trick would only buy them a few seconds more.

Lucy peered through the broken pane of a window to the side and could see the flashes of the pirate's guns and the numbing light of dark power at play.

Suddenly the golem disintegrated with a mighty whoosh. His waters and debris rushed backward like a wave that hit the weakened Savannah full in the face, cutting her head.

Seeing her sister hurt stirred Lucy into angered action, and instinctively rubbing the wings of the Ravenring with her thumb, her complexion turned dark as she sent a nightmarish maelstrom of flying creatures into the heart of the chaos.

As Alice flowed with the slipstream of her minions into the

cottage, the scene that greeted her was of carnage. Madame Rebecca and pirate Stanley were stuck in sticky webbing, pinned to a wall. Stanley was covered in blood and not moving.

Ziggy was lying on the floor, unarmed, clutching his face.

Meanwhile Nelson, the pirate leader, his blade flashing, slashing and darting, was in a bitter duel with an old crone, surprisingly strong and nimble for her age. Her arms were a flurry of shadow and it was clear from her grin that, despite his undoubted dexterity with his sword, she was enjoying the contest, cackling under her breath and toying with him. The denizens of the Ravenring obscured the fight. But it was clear she was prolonging the thrill like spiteful cat with mouse, saving the final thrust from her magical staff which she seemingly could take at will.

Nelson's efforts, as well as the swirling and swooping bats, crows and ravens had, however, bought their gang some time. Despite her confident manner, the crone was clearly distracted by the dark mob and unable to wield staff and spell at once.

Looking to the front door, Lucy could see the Druid Brinn on his hands and knees. He was crumpled behind a faint magical shield, in a pool of blood, power now faded like his complexion, to a very pale blue.

Somehow Lucy knew what to do.

As Brinn's power finally crackled out, she quickly darted beside him. She then rapidly re-sealed the doorway using the dark force of her Ravenring, much in the same way as she had unsealed the entrance the day before.

A cloak of transparent black mist was erected before them and this brought a frustrated scream from the witch, distracted by her fight.

A deft but impatient twirl of her staff knocked the rapier from the pirate's hands, sending it clattering to the floor. But Nelson tucked and rolled in time to avoid the terminal blow which glanced off his shoulder instead, drawing a shriek of pain.

Considering him now finished, the witch turned to survey Lucy's handiwork. But from the doorway Savannah caught the pirate's eye and slid something to him along the dusty wooden floor.

Having assessed the situation, the wytch re-focused and turned back to Nelson with a wicked grin. Opting to terminate her work with him, she raised her staff above her head in both hands. The incantation she was uttering sounded like a terrible curse and blue flames were leaping about her cold, hard hands. She clearly intended to end his constant influence on their fate now and for all time.

Although the sight of the witch was terrifying to behold, this was the opening the shrewd pirate prince had been looking for.

Ignoring the pain in his arm, contrary to her expectations, he forced his battered body forward as she thrust. Using her momentum, he now lunged with the strange cold knife that had somehow found its way into his hands. As luck would have it, he managed to hit home. The jade blade bit hungrily into the folds of the old crone's death-black robes, as if it had a hungry grudge of its own. It bit home. A flash of arching light instantly threw the pirate backward and he landed in a tangled, lifeless heap. But not before his opponent shrieked in panic and pain again.

This time the witch let out a filthy, shrill cry that signalled her fear and frustration. Her dark spell had been broken, by the magic in the unexpected blade and a pulse of agony that bent her in two.

Those still conscious in the cottage were able to gulp down a desperate breath or two. But the respite didn't last long.

Hatred driving her on, the sea wytch reeled. She was about to turn on Savannah, her granddaughter who had brought the Athame. Then her black eyes flashed from wild anger to abject disbelief.

A giant form now appeared in the magic archway. Its shadow suddenly filling the room, casting a longer shade in the gloom.

"I have come for you, Mother," a curiously feminine voice boomed from that huge mouth.

"Enough now. You have done enough. This cruelty must end, and it will end this day."

Despite her sightless eyes, the giant walked straight to their tormentor, as if guided by another light.

"How dare you defy me, child," the witch screamed as the great hands reached for her. But, power spent and dulled by the potion of tears which had broken in her pocket, nothing she could muster now slowed the progress of her daughter.

"This ending I have seen, Mother. It is the ending I have been concealing from you, and so it must now be."

Her silhouette crackling with the light and dark magic that was swirling around the cramped space, the gentle giant girl scooped the screaming heap of rags and ancient dusty flesh into her great arms.

Seemingly oblivious to the weak curses, she then turned, unceremoniously, as if fearing to pause and disappeared relentlessly back down the tunnel dumb to the increasingly desperate screams her mother continued to hurl.

Finally, to the shock of those still conscious enough to take it all in, the archway sealed itself behind them, corners melting into the mud, entombing both the other side of the veil for good.

Looking on in silence, the battered band of friends were left with the haunting sight and sounds of water swirling down a deep, dark drain. And just above that noise, the last thing they heard was a long, drawn-out, soul-destroying wail of a certain shallow soul being dragged to hell, very much against its iron will.

Back at the African cave, the chameleon had now climbed onto Alice's shoulder as if it belonged there. This was much to her delight, of course, and the great fascination of the family.

They were so enchanted by its quirky character, that they almost missed the fact that part of the giant world map had now started throbbing noticeably, emitting a golden aura that warmed the darkness.

"Look," said Elouisa, "a change is taking place in the magical network. It is like the winds of fate have shifted."

The lights on the map spread to Africa, causing them all to freeze in their tracks and stare. The amethyst crystals began to glow and then vibrate, humming audibly.

A blinding flash of light caused them all to cover their eyes instinctively. The Tokoloshe vanished into the darker recesses and Henry felt compelled to run in from where he had been keeping watch outside.

It now dawned on them that they were witnessing a message. The goddess was telling them something afresh. That the latest threat wasn't going to come from outside this time, but very much from within.

When their eyes adjusted to the light show, they were momentarily stunned once more. For now, in front of them, strolling casually from the back of the cave, eyes blinking, was what appeared to be the beautiful form of their own darling Lucy.

She sprinted gleefully forward upon seeing them, half-thrilled and half-terrified, arms thrown wide in a very Lucy-like way.

Just a little way behind her was Savannah.

The lithe but sleight figure, however, was struggling to support an old and it would appear very sick man. His skin was brittle and white and he was bedecked in bloodied, ancient robes that gave him the appearance of an Egyptian mummy.

"Children?" said Elouisa, as puzzled as they were pleased to see her.

But there was little time for explanations.

Savannah gestured to the men for help and they took the fragile, aged casualty in hand between them, placing him tenderly with his back to the goddess statue.

Elouisa, however, suddenly went very, very quiet.

"What is it?" asked James, torn between caring for the old man and his wife's stunned reaction.

She paused and then answered him slowly.

"James, don't you recognise him?"

He stared at her blankly.

"James, this, this man...Do you not see the likeness?"

Seconds of silence lasted minutes.

"HE is...family. He is my father!"

Despite his pain, a flicker of acknowledgement passed over the old Druid's face, recognising a voice he loved.

Ignoring the unfolding drama, Moses and the sangoma set to attending to the injured man. His dark wound was now weeping a yellowy poison Moses recognised and it was clearly infecting his system.

"This is not good news. The dark magic has leeched into his injury, my friend," said Moses, looking up at Eloisa's emotion-racked face as she held her father's hand, his health visibly draining away.

"Like the poison we saw earlier in you, it is as if he has been struck by the venom of the Mamba snake."

"I could try a potion...something...anything," she said frantically searching for answers.

"No," answered Brinn, in a weak voice, dismissing all protest with the wave of a weak hand.

"The evil has gone too deep," he croaked. "It is my time."

All fell silent, knowing the value and therefore the cost of these muffled words.

"Just seeing your face again, my daughter, and your children...has been enough for..." but his voice trailed off.

"No, no, no!" she screamed.

A ripple of shock passed over the children, who were not

accustomed to seeing their composed mother lose her self-control in this way.

Her quiet sobs echoed dully round the unanswering cave.

But even in this, the darkest of moments, Holly looked up and noticed another change happening to the statue.

Colour was starting to bleed into the soapstone. The goddess's flesh was gaining pigment and texture as each of the artefacts about her person lit up in turn.

The Willowand and Rubyrobe on the statue glowed still and soon the Moonstone brought the necklace to life entirely. On her finger the Ravenring began to light up until, finally, at the tail of this magical chain, about the goddess's belt, what Savannah recognised as the Jade Athame started pulsing with an ancient force.

While they were all distracted by this latest mystical metamorphosis, nobody noticed that the little chameleon had made its slow and steady way down to the fast-fading Brinn.

It soon perched purposefully on his chest. Then, incredibly, it appeared to fold its legs over the very spot where his old heart was just beating, albeit faintly.

Time seemed to freeze as the girls held his hand and they all impotently watched the last life drain from the old man's limp body as the shadows lengthened on the cave walls.

Yet as the children succumbed to tears, while the old man slipped from them; rather comically, like a perched owl asleep in the dark woods, the druid unexpectedly opened one misty eye. Then from somewhere he summoned a crack-toothed smile.

Elouisa, who was still at his side, gently greeted him again, in hushed tones, her face filled with tears, but now of hope more than grief.

"Father. Father? How? Are you….?"

The tired old man said nothing. Saving his breath.

Instead, he reached out and beckoned all the children closer to him while the rest of the family looked on.

Then he turned his face to the cave entrance.

Outside, beyond the womb of the sacred place, a dramatic backdrop to this touching African scene had been unfolding steadily.

As if following nature's cue, for the first time in almost a decade, the wispy clouds had gathered strength in numbers. Now what they promised was a long-neglected blessing for the thirsty earth.

The songbirds circled in joyful anticipation, insects danced and Africa's shy wildlife cavorted skittishly sensing what was about to happen.

Then, with a roar in the clouds and a clap of thunder, the bubble of tension suddenly burst, the clouds gave way and the sky parted.

All about the mouth of the sanctuary, the red desert opened its parched lips to the deluge. With the vigour of a lapping deer, the ancient land joined the shy animals and the patient plants in soaking up the welcome, nourishing, healing rain.

It was clear to all who witnessed it, whether from this world or beyond the veil, that this long-awaited desert storm was a blessing. They had waited for this for generations and the rain was bringing the promise of new life, fresh beginnings and the bounty of the next adventure.

A new journey was clearly pending, for this family. And it would be beyond this African horizon or their island home. When it happened, it would be an exploration of far-flung climes and the remaining corners of the world.

But for now, the watching Africans especially, rejoiced at the magic of this scene, as they too beheld the glory that was spreading from the re-discovered goddess.

So it was that with arms opened wide, they welcomed the future. They drenched their bodies in the cleansing, revitalising water that was surely heaven sent. They smiled together and they wept with joy.

ABOUT THE AUTHOR

English author Ian P Buckingham is widely published across a range of genres and mediums. A bit of a modern renaissance man, his work spans high-brow business books on brand and communication as well as magical adventure stories for children and young adults.

Winner of various creative writing prizes throughout his career and education in Africa and England, he has studied at Harvard as well as the University of Leeds where he also specialised in children's and Commonwealth literature.

Ian has edited several publications including poetry and creative writing magazines and has written, produced and directed plays.

A proud father of two daughters (the muses for the important work) and a passionate shared parenting advocate, when not writing or roaming Britain's coastline and forests, Ian is a prominent management consultant and MBA lecturer, championing the crucial role of great stories in life generally, no matter the age of the reader.

Other books by Ian P Buckingham:
The Changeling Saga Book One: Legend of the Lost

For details of our other books, or to submit your own manuscript please visit www.green-cat.shop

GREEN CAT BOOKS

Printed in Great Britain
by Amazon

71832725R00154